WHO ARE THE RECORD BREAKERS?

They are the fastest men on the basepaths. They are the pitchers who can't be beat. They are the hitters who slug the ball out of the park, or who set up amazing streaks of consecutive hits. They are the stars of the game—they make it our national pastime! You are going to love reading about the amazing things that the very best players on the diamond have done.

Go ahead, have a ball with . . .

BASEBALL'S RECORD BREAKERS

Books by Bill Gutman

Sports Illustrated: BASEBALL'S RECORD BREAKERS
Sports Illustrated: GREAT MOMENTS IN BASEBALL
Sports Illustrated: GREAT MOMENTS IN PRO FOOTBALL
Sports Illustrated: PRO FOOTBALL'S RECORD BREAKERS
Sports Illustrated: STRANGE AND AMAZING BASEBALL
   STORIES
Sports Illustrated: STRANGE AND AMAZING FOOTBALL
   STORIES
BASEBALL SUPER TEAMS
BASEBALL'S HOT NEW STARS
BO JACKSON: A BIOGRAPHY
FOOTBALL SUPER TEAMS
GREAT SPORTS UPSETS
GREAT SPORTS UPSETS 2
MICHAEL JORDAN: A BIOGRAPHY
PRO SPORTS CHAMPIONS
STRANGE AND AMAZING WRESTLING STORIES

Available from ARCHWAY Paperbacks

BASEBALL'S RECORD BREAKERS

Bill Gutman

AN ARCHWAY PAPERBACK
Published by POCKET BOOKS
New York   London   Toronto   Sydney   Tokyo   Singapore

Photos courtesy of *Sports Illustrated* © Time Inc.: John Iacono:
pp. 12, 17; Chuck Solomon: pp. 40 (top), 43, 116; John D. Hanlon:
p. 40 (bottom); Walter Iooss Jr.: pp. 61, 77; Ronald C. Modra: p. 66;
Tony Triolo: pp. 96, 101. Photos on pp. 7, 32, 83, 85, 93, 106, 118
courtesy of AP/Wide World Photos.

AN ARCHWAY PAPERBACK *Original*

An Archway Paperback published by
POCKET BOOKS, a division of Simon & Schuster Inc.
1230 Avenue of the Americas, New York, NY 10020

ISBN: 0-671-70217-3

First Archway Paperback printing March 1988

13 12 11 10 9 8 7 6 5

AN ARCHWAY PAPERBACK and colophon are
registered trademarks of Simon & Schuster Inc.

SPORTS ILLUSTRATED is a registered trademark
of Time Inc.

Printed in the U.S.A.

IL 5+

Contents

The Streak

There's an old sports axiom that says, simply, *records are made to be broken!* Set a record, no matter how great, and someday someone is going to come along and break it. As a rule, the axiom is an accurate one. Just apply it to the National Pastime, for instance. There have been a number of great, long-standing records, once considered unbreakable, that have fallen in the past several decades.

The legendary Babe Ruth no longer holds the home-run records for a season and career. His 60 and 714, perhaps the most recognizable numbers in the game, were surpassed by Roger Maris' 61 and Henry Aaron's 755. When Sandy Koufax set a new season's strikeout mark of 382 in 1965, it was thought the record would stand for years. But in 1973, just eight years later, fireballer Nolan Ryan whiffed 383. And in 1985, the great Pete Rose surpassed Hall of Famer Ty Cobb's lifetime mark of 4,191 base hits, another record many thought would never be broken.

So the records continue to fall. But there are still a few that people think will defeat the axiom and never be broken. Though history may say otherwise, some baseball romantics still like to hope. And one of the first records mentioned in this context is almost always "The Streak."

Baseball fans need no further explanation. The streak refers to an incredible record set back in 1941 by Joseph Paul DiMaggio, better known as Joe D., DiMag, or the Yankee Clipper. Over a two-month period that year, Joe D. had one or more hits in 56 consecutive games, setting a standard that has rarely been approached in the more than four decades that have passed since.

Why is a lengthy hitting streak such a difficult thing to maintain? It's simple. There are so many different ways it can end, even if the player is swinging a hot bat. Suppose the pitcher decides to work around the hitter. A couple of walks and it's over. Or suppose the hitter stings the ball each time up—only right at a fielder. It's over. What if a couple of fielders turn in spectacular plays on the hitter? The streak ends.

And there is the self-imposed pressure of knowing you have to get that one hit every game to keep it going. Many hitters will tense up, especially if they don't hit safely their first or second trips to the plate. Then forget it. So for Joe DiMaggio to hit safely in 56 straight games, well, that's surely a streak to remember.

DiMag was just twenty-six years old when the 1941 season opened, but he was already in his sixth season with the Bronx Bombers. By that time, he had established himself as the superstar to carry on the tradition started by Babe Ruth and Lou Gehrig. Patrolling centerfield with speed and grace, DiMaggio was a complete ballplayer who had already won an American League batting title with a .381 mark in 1939, had taken a home-run crown with 46 in 1937, and had driven home 167 runs that same year. That's the kind of player he was.

There was also some precedent for DiMag going on a sustained hitting streak. As an eighteen-year-old playing for the San Francisco Seals in the Pacific Coast League in 1933, young Joe D. astounded West Coast fans by hitting safely in 61 straight games. Two years later, he hit a whopping .398 for the Seals, banging out 270 hits in a 172-game schedule. He was the darling of the West Coast, which was still more than two decades away from having a major league team.

The big leagues couldn't ignore a ballplayer of his caliber, however, and it was the Yankees who had bought his contract from San Francisco. DiMag was a smash right from his rookie year, and the rest, as they say, is history. That history was being created by Joe's mighty bat and all-around ability, and when 1941 began he was already an established and acknowledged superstar.

Two weeks into the season Joe was hitting a sizzling .528, and the Yanks seemed ready to regain the American League pennant they had lost to Detroit the previous year. But then DiMag went into a slump, and as he himself said, "I couldn't buy a hit." And as the

Clipper slumped, so did the Yanks. By mid-May the team was at 14–14. Then on May 15, Joe slammed a first-inning single, but went hitless the rest of the way as the Bronx Bombers fell below .500. Little did anyone know then, but that hit was the start of something very big.

The next day Joe homered, then led off the ninth with a triple that keyed a comeback win for his team. After that, both Joe and the Yanks picked up the pace. That was expected, and about two weeks later, a local newsman ended his game story with this sentence:

DiMaggio has now hit safely in 18 straight games.

Still nothing to get excited about, except for the fact that the Yankee Clipper was once again carrying the team. Hitting streaks usually don't draw much notice until they reach the 20 or 25 game mark. In 1941, the post-1900 mark was 41 straight games, set by the great George Sisler. Ty Cobb had once hit in 40 straight, and prior to 1900, another outstanding hitter, Wee Willie Keeler, ran a streak of 44 straight games. It seemed that the longest hitting streaks were only accomplished by quality hitters.

DiMag continued to get hits, and when the streak reached 25 games, he began thinking about it for the first time. He wasn't thinking about the all-time record, but about the Yankee club record, which was 29 games, set by Roger Peckinpaugh and equaled by Earle Combs. Joe tied that with a fifth-inning double against Cleveland on June 16. The next day against Chicago, Joe went for a new Yankee record.

He was hitless, however, when he came to bat in the seventh inning. Digging in, he hit the ball hard, but right in the direction of shortstop Luke Appling. At the last second, the ball took a high hop and bounced off Appling's shoulder. When he picked it up and fired to first, Joe had already crossed the bag. DiMag and everyone else looked to the press box to see how official scorer Dan Daniel would call it.

Base hit! Daniel felt the bad hop made it almost impossible for Appling to make the play. Sure, it was luck, but a little luck never hurt anyone, and is part of nearly every great achievement. As Joe himself said, after the game:

"Dan Daniel is an honest man who wouldn't give you a thing you didn't deserve. If you were going for a record, *you* have to break it. You get no gifts from him and that's the way it should be."

From there, Joe quickly rolled it up to 35 games, and now the entire baseball world began focusing on the Yankee Clipper. Sisler's record was well within reach and the pressure began to mount. Now, each opposing pitcher wanted to be the guy who stopped DiMaggio, and they bore down each time he came to the plate. There was added pressure for DiMag also, because as an intensely private and shy man, he was now thrust into the limelight as never before. It wasn't always easy to handle.

He had another close call in game 36, slamming a solid single in his final at bat in the bottom of the eighth. It was another case where a pitcher could have simply thrown four wide pitches and walked him, ending the streak. But out of respect for Joe, most pitchers challenged him and tried to stop him with their best stuff.

The pressure continued to mount and Joe DiMaggio continued to hit. On June 28, he cracked a single off Johnny Babich of Philadelphia, giving him a streak of 40 straight games and bringing him within one game of George Sisler. And Sisler himself said if anyone broke his record, he would want it to be DiMag.

"The guy is a great natural ballplayer and great hitter," Sisler said. "That makes the streak real, no lucky fluke, believe me."

A doubleheader in Washington, on June 29, gave DiMag a chance to tie and break the record in one afternoon. With the suspense building in game one, Joe D. went hitless until the sixth inning. Then, facing knuckleballer Dutch Leonard, the Yankee Clipper picked out a floater and slammed a ringing double to left. He had tied the mark at 41.

But in the clubhouse between games, a crisis arose. Someone walked off with Joe's favorite bat, the one he had been using throughout the streak. Now, he had to go into what was perhaps the biggest game of his life with a borrowed bat. Like most ballplayers, Joe was somewhat superstitious and didn't like the idea of losing his favorite bat at such a crucial time. But he knew he had to go on, so he borrowed a piece of lumber from Tommy Henrich and went out to try to break the record.

A happy Joe DiMaggio displays a collection of his favorite bats after extending his record hitting streak to 56 consecutive games on July 16, 1941. The following day the streak was finally stopped.

By the seventh inning he was still hitless and the crowd was getting edgy. So was Joe, but he didn't show it as he came up to face Arnold Anderson. Standing deep in the box on the right side, bat held high as always, he concentrated on the pitcher. The stride and the picture-perfect swing were all familiar to Yankee fans. So was the result. Another solid single to left and this time a new record. DiMag had hit safely in his 42nd consecutive game.

If Joe thought that would take the pressure off, it didn't. Now, everyone wanted to see just how far the Yankee Clipper could go. Keeler's all-time record of 44 was next, and Joe sailed past. It almost seemed as if the streak would never end. When Joe passed the 50-game mark, his record was already being hailed as one of the best of all-time. On July 16, he smacked out three hits against two Cleveland pitchers to run his streak to 56 straight games.

Then came game 57. Joe's bat had been blazing. Over the past 10 games he had 23 hits in 40 at-bats for an incredible .575 average. Facing Cleveland lefty Al Smith, Joe tagged the ball in both his first and third at-bats. But both times Indians third baseman Ken Keltner made brilliant stops and threw DiMag out at first. On his second chance at bat, Joe walked. When he came up in the eighth, he was facing righthander Jim Bagby, and once again the streak was on the line.

Joe waited intently, got his pitch, and swung. Once more he connected solidly, but his luck had run out. He hit a smash at shortstop Lou Boudreau, who gloved it, and went to second to start a bang-bang doubleplay. Joe was out and the streak was over. At last.

"I can't say I'm glad it's over," Joe said after the game. "I wanted it to go on as long as it could. But now that it's over, I just want to keep helping the Yanks to win ballgames."

Talking about his streak years later, Joe reiterated how he wanted it to keep going, admitting, "I think I wanted it to go on forever."

To many fans in 1941, it seemed as if it did. During the streak, Joe blazed away at a .408 pace, with 91 hits in 223 at-bats. He clubbed 15 homers, drove home 55 runs, and struck out only seven times. His streak had received so much attention that Boston's great slugger, Ted Williams, batted .418 over the span of Joe's streak and no one noticed. Williams would hit .406 in 1941, but DiMag, with his .357 final average and league-leading 125 RBIs, was voted the league's Most Valuable Player after the season ended.

Joe DiMaggio's 56-game hitting streak was viewed as a sterling achievement back when it happened, and it's viewed as an even greater achievement today. In all the intervening years, very few players have really threatened the record, and only one has caused a media stir that rivaled that given to DiMag.

Oh, yes, there might be some people wondering just what would have happened if Ken Keltner had not made those great plays so long ago and Joe had hit safely in a 57th game. Well, right after he was stopped, the Yankee Clipper pulled himself together and hit safely in 17 more. So if Keltner had not made the play, Joe would have had a streak of 74 straight games. That's how good he was.

Rose Challenges DiMag

In the years following 1941, DiMaggio's hitting streak always stayed in the news. Whenever a big-leaguer put together a streak that reached 20 or 25 games, the stories about Joe D.'s great standard surfaced again, along with speculation about the streaking player making a challenge. But most times the streak ended somewhere between 20 and 30 games, reminding baseball fans just how great and how unreachable DiMag's mark was.

One streak that got a bit more attention occurred in 1945, when the Boston Braves' Tommy Holmes took a hitting streak past 30 games. Once again the feats of Cobb, Sisler, Wee Willie Keeler, and ultimately DiMaggio were recalled. Holmes finally stalled at 37, setting a new modern National League record along the way but falling far short of the Clipper.

Let's go to 1978. Once again DiMag's mark seemed among the safest of records. At the outset of the season, much attention was focused on one of the greatest of the modern players, Pete Rose of the Cincinnati Reds. Rose was a throwback, a hustling player who wouldn't hesitate to dirty his uniform and put his body on the line to win a ballgame. He was also talented, a switch hitter who rarely missed a game, hit the ball to all fields, and was versatile enough to play both the infield and outfield on defense.

In 1963, Rose was a twenty-two-year-old rookie who quickly earned the nickname of Charley Hustle. Two years later he had his first .300 season, batting .312 with 209 hits in the process. He was off and running, and he never stopped. A member of the awesome Big Red Machine of the middle 1970s, Pete helped the Cincy team into the World Series four times. The club that won it all in 1975 and 1976 is considered by many as one of the best of all time, with names like Bench, Morgan, Foster, Griffey, Perez, Concepcion, and Pete Rose.

The team was aging a bit when 1978 began, but the thirty-seven-year-old Rose showed no signs of slowing down. And when the year started, baseball people were anticipating another milestone for Pete. He was just 34 hits short of 3,000 for his career, a mark reached by only a handful of great players. On the night of May 5, Pete made the magical moment. He slammed out two hits off Montreal's Steve Rogers to become only the thirteenth player in big-league history to reach 3,000. It seemed to most observers that Rose had already provided the highlight of the year. But they were wrong. Oh, were they wrong.

After the early excitement caused by Pete's 3,000th hit, the Reds began to falter. Joe Morgan, for one, was playing with torn stomach muscles, and pitcher Tom

Pete Rose, old "Charley Hustle" himself, smacks out still another base hit. Rose captured the fancy of the baseball world in 1978 when he made a run at Joe DiMaggio's 56-game hitting streak. Though Rose was stopped at 44, baseball's all-time hit leader joined Wee Willie Keeler with the second longest streak in baseball history.

Seaver, who had won 14 games for the Reds after coming over from the Mets the year before, couldn't seem to regain his form. And perhaps most surprisingly, Pete Rose was in a batting slump.

By June 13, his average was down to .267, not nearly a Rose figure, and he had just five hits in his last 44 at-bats. That comes out to an average of .114. As with any player in his late thirties, the slump brought the usual question. Had he lost it? Had age caught up with him suddenly and cruelly? Pete answered the only way he knew how.

On June 14, he pounded out a pair of hits off Dave Roberts of the Cubs. In the next game, he got two more, and in the game after that he repeated with another pair of safeties. With six hits in 12 trips, it looked as if his slump was over. But it was more than that. Pete Rose was once again about to turn the baseball world into his own personal stage.

The hitting spree continued, with Pete banging them out game after game. In a June 24 tilt against the Dodgers, he slammed out four hits in five trips. It was the ninth straight game in which he had hit safely, and more importantly, the team was winning again. At this point, however, no one really considered his spree a streak. But by June 30, he had run it to 16, and on July 4, when he banged out a hit against J. R. Richard of Houston, he made it 20 in a row.

Now, it was a streak, though at 20 games, real interest was still mild, and no one really mentioned the DiMaggio record. In fact, if it were anyone but Pete Rose, it would hardly be mentioned at all. But Charley Hustle had a way of making headlines, not to speak of records, as well. So the reporters sought him out and, as usual, Pete Rose was all too happy to oblige them.

"I can't say how it got started," he said. "It was almost an accident. I'm a consistent player and I always hit. So I started to get some hits and they kept

13

falling during each game. Suddenly, it became a streak."

A streak it was, all right, because Pete Rose continued to hit. By July 17, he had hit in 30 straight, and now the buzzing began. After all, he was just seven games behind Tommy Holmes' National League record. And someone else pointed out that there had only been 18 hitting streaks of 30 or more games since 1900. So Pete was moving into elite company. But at 30 games, there was still little mention of the veteran chasing or catching DiMaggio at 56. But the questions were beginning.

One of the first things any player feels when he arrives in possible record-breaking territory is the pressure. It comes from the fans, the media, sometimes teammates, and most always from within. Pressure can help a player, but it can also hurt him. In Pete's case, it always helped, because he thrived on it. His manager, Sparky Anderson, confirmed just that.

"The pressure won't get to Pete," Anderson said. "In fact, he loves it, just like he loves the World Series, the playoffs, or the All-Star Game. The more attention he gets, the better. He lives for this."

Indeed, he did. No matter how many questions he was asked, Pete answered patiently, honestly, and often with humor, citing statistics from the past and pieces of baseball trivia that few players knew. And on the field he was showing all the experience and skill acquired during a long career.

In the thirty-second game, the Phils were holding

him hitless when he came up for probably his final plate appearance in the ninth inning. With big Ron Reed on the mound, Pete dropped a perfect bunt down the third-base line and beat it out. Base hit. The next night he legged out a hit to second base to run his streak to 33 games. Then on July 23, Pete smacked another pair of hits against Montreal to run his streak to 36 games. The excitement was really building.

As the Reds traveled to New York for a series against the Mets, Pete was just a game away from tying Holmes' record. And by this time, there were some people saying that if anyone could catch Joe DiMaggio, it was Pete Rose. After all, he was a contact hitter, a switch hitter, and a resourceful hitter. He didn't strike out much, and he wasn't averse to bunting when necessary.

Much to Pete's surprise, the huge crowd at Shea Stadium was cheering wildly for a man they considered an old and long-standing enemy. But facing tough right-hander Pat Zachry, a former teammate, proved no easy task. In his first two at-bats, Pete lofted lazy flies to the outfield. The next time he bounced into a fielder's choice. When he came up for the fourth time in the seventh inning, it was all on the line once again. He might not get another chance.

Once again Pete thought about bunting to keep the streak going. He tried it on Zachry's first pitch, but fouled the ball off. After taking a pitch for a ball, Pete decided to swing away, and he hit a liner to left. The crowd held its collective breath as leftfielder Steve

Henderson charged in. But the ball dropped in front of him for a clean single. Rose had 37 straight and a standing ovation.

"Pressure situations are fun," he said, again, after the game. "When people are urging me on, I can do things that are impossible sometimes."

The next night there was even more pressure, because with another hit Pete would have the National League record. Facing Mets' righthander Craig Swan, he flied out to left his first time up. But when he came up again in the third, he promptly lined a hit past the shortstop. He had done it, 38 straight games. Now the big question was whether he could catch Joe D.

"I'm ready to continue," Pete said. "DiMaggio is out there by himself, but I'm hitting the ball good and I've got half the house built. So now I've got to go on and build the rest."

There was little doubt that Pete welcomed the challenge of a record even as awesome as DiMaggio's. One night later he slammed a fifth-inning double off Nino Espinosa, then as the Reds faced Philadelphia, he whacked a third-inning two-bagger off Randy Lerch to run his streak to 40 games. And since Pete was a walking encyclopedia of baseball knowledge, he was well aware that he had just tied the best of the great Ty Cobb.

In the second game of that doubleheader he hit the ball hard twice for outs. So the third time he dropped a nifty bunt down third for another base hit and his forty-first straight. He had now pulled even with another

Hats off to a record. Cincinnati's Pete Rose waves to the Shea Stadium crowd in New York after setting a new National League record by hitting safely in his 38th straight game in 1978. With him is the former record holder, Tommy Holmes.

Hall of Famer, George Sisler. Phillies third baseman Mike Schmidt, an outstanding fielder, had been victimized twice by Pete's bunts during the streak. He could only marvel at the cool of the veteran.

"Pete's never bunted on me before," Schmidt said. "Then he lays down two perfect ones with all that pressure on him. I've really got to respect him. He's the epitome of concentration, and he's turned into my idol."

Now Pete seemed more loose and relaxed than ever. He banged out three hits in the third game against

Philly, then in the finale slapped a fifth-inning single to run his skein to 43 straight. When asked about catching DiMag, Pete was ready with the one-liners.

"Right now I'm going after Sidney Stonestreet's 48-game streak," he told a disbelieving press corps. "You've probably never heard of him. I can understand that, since I just made him up."

Atlanta was the next stop and knuckleballer Phil Niekro the next pitcher to try to stop Pete Rose. Rose walked his first time up, lined out his second. But, in the sixth inning, Rose smacked a base hit to make it 44. He had pulled even with Wee Willie Keeler for the second longest hitting streak in all of baseball history. A hit the next night against rookie lefthander Larry McWilliams would put Pete all by himself in the number-two spot with only DiMaggio ahead of him.

But suddenly his luck ran out. He walked the first time up. Next time he got his pitch and lashed a liner back through the box. It looked like a sure hit, but pitcher McWilliams stuck out his glove with a reflex action and made a backhanded grab. In the fifth, Pete hit a hard one-hopper, but right to the shortstop. He was hitless in three trips and time was getting short.

In the seventh, reliever Gene Garber was on the mound and Pete hit another line shot. Only this one was speared by third sacker Bob Horner who turned it into a doubleplay. It sure looked as if Lady Luck had taken a vacation. Now the question was, would Pete get still another chance?

He did in the ninth. He fouled off a bunt attempt,

then worked the count to two and two. Garber threw a change and Pete swung . . . and missed! Strike three. He walked slowly back toward the dugout. The fans at Atlanta and the millions more watching on a special national television hookup knew at the same time, as did Pete. The streak was over at 44 games.

Some players might be glad the pressure was off, that it had ended. Not Pete Rose.

"I'm not relieved," he said. "In fact, I'm teed off. I wish it could go on forever. It's been exciting and enjoyable. I feel as if I've lost my best friend."

Candid as always, Pete would have liked nothing better than to have broken DiMag's record. As it was, he had come closer than any player since the mark was set. In the 44 games, he had 70 hits in 182 trips for a .385 average, and he brought his own average up from .267 to .316. It was now another typical Rose season.

Besides playing his usual fiery brand of winning baseball, he had created an electricity that the entire country could share. He had made a real run at one of the greatest baseball records ever set, one of the few records many feel is unbreakable. And though he fell short, Pete Rose won over a whole new legion of fans who would continue to watch him in the ensuing years as he set many great records of his own.

The Ultimate Contact Hitter

When Pete Rose struck out to end his 44-game hitting streak, it surprised some people. Not that the streak had ended. That had to happen. But as a contact hitter, Pete did not strike out too often. Yet there was once a major leaguer who struck out so few times that he'd make Pete Rose or anyone else look like a strikeout king.

His name was Joe Sewell and he played for Cleveland and the New York Yankees from 1920 to 1933. Sewell was not just your run-of-the-mill ballplayer or a part-timer. He was one of the stars of his day, an infielder who rarely missed a game for nine straight years, playing in more than 150 games each season. So you know he got his at-bats.

He was a fine hitter, all right, compiling a .300 or better average in 10 of his 14 big-league seasons, with a high of .353 in 1923. For his career, which spanned 1,902 games, Joe Sewell compiled a solid lifetime average of .312. His outstanding career was fully recognized in 1977 when he was elected to baseball's Hall of Fame.

But in addition to all that, Joe Sewell set several records that will be very difficult to top, and they have to do with striking out. In two separate seasons, 1925 and 1929, playing the entire schedule, Joe Sewell struck out just four times. Incredible! Just eight strike-outs in 307 games. It almost sounds impossible.

That isn't all. Joe Sewell also holds the record for the fewest strikeouts for a career. In fourteen years he fanned a total of 114 times. That averages out to barely over eight strikeouts a season. And for his career, Sewell whiffed an average of just once in 63 at-bats, another record. By comparison, Joe DiMaggio struck out once in every 18.48 at-bats, and another great slugger, Mickey Mantle, fanned once in every 4.74 at-bats.

In 1930, a White Sox pitcher named Pat Caraway accomplished the near impossible. He struck out Joe Sewell twice in one game. The date was May 26, less than two months into the season. Mark it well. Because for the rest of the year, through June, July, August, and September, Joe Sewell did not strike out again, not once, not a single time.

That was Joe Sewell, a record breaker for sure. It would surely be interesting to see how the contact-making Sewell would fare against the great strikeout pitchers of today, guys like Roger Clemens, Mike Scott, Nolan Ryan, and Dwight Gooden. Could they fan Joe Sewell? Unfortunately, we can only guess, or leave it to the computers. But wouldn't the real thing be fun?

Record-breaking Tie

Baseball records are interesting in many ways. It takes some players an entire career, sometimes twenty years, to set a mark, only to see it broken in their lifetimes. Others take a season, while a few set their records in a single day. But there was once a case where two players set the same record in one day, and it's a record that hasn't been broken in nearly seventy years. In fact, it may never be broken.

It happened on May 1, 1920, as the old Boston Braves got set to meet the old Brooklyn Dodgers. Officially, the team was the "Robins," but already they were known as the Dodgers. The Braves had veteran Joe Oeschger on the mound that day, while Brooklyn countered with another vet, Leon Cadore. Both pitchers would close out mediocre careers with more losses than wins. But on this cool May afternoon in 1920, each one would make baseball history.

It was apparent from the start that both pitchers had their good stuff. At the end of six innings the score was tied at one run each and the game was zipping right along. After nine it was still 1–1 and zipping right along. After 15 innings the score was still deadlocked at one each. Both Oeschger and Cadore were continuing on the mound, each throwing easily and showing no signs of fatigue.

Before long the game passed the 20-inning mark and the players and fans began to wonder if it would ever end. The two pitchers remained in control, setting the opposition down quickly. Though relief pitchers weren't used too often in those days, you just had to wonder just how far the starters could go.

The answer came six innings later. That's when the game had to be called because of darkness. The score was still tied, and Joe Oeschger and Leon Cadore were still pitching. Each had completed 26 innings of one-run ball when the game was called. It was baseball's longest game in terms of innings, a mark that still stands today.

So does the 26 innings pitched by both Oeschger and Cadore. The former gave up just nine hits, walked three, and fanned four, while the latter yielded 15 hits, walked five, and struck out eight. Yet neither got a victory, or picked up a loss. Their record-breaking performance went into the books as nothing more than a tie.

Yet it's a record that will undoubtedly continue to stand. Even if there was a pitcher today capable of throwing 26 innings, no manager in his right mind would allow it. The philosophy of pitching has changed and relief specialists abound everywhere. It's even rare to see a starter continue into extra innings. But in 1920, Joe Oeschger and Leon Cadore did it, nearly pitching the equivalent of three full games. That's a record, all right.

Two for the Price of One

When Oeschger and Cadore set their 26-inning record, it was totally unexpected. But there was a time when a pitcher woke up to a new day knowing he was expected to pitch both ends of a doubleheader. It didn't happen very often, and most of the cases were in the early days of the century. But there was one pitcher who seemed to excel at pitching doubleheaders and he's remembered for it even today.

His name was Joe McGinnity and his nickname was "Iron Man." That should say something right there. He was good enough to win 247 games in a ten-year career that lasted from 1899 to 1908, and his overall performance got him elected to baseball's Hall of Fame in 1946. Born in 1871, McGinnity got an unusually late start, breaking in when he was already twenty-eight years old. That explains his relatively short career.

But the Iron Man made up for lost time in his performance, often pitching close to 50 games a year. And when they needed someone to pitch two, he was always ready. It first happened in 1901, when McGinnity was pitching for Baltimore of the new American League. When the pitching got a little thin in September, the Iron Man began to build his reputation.

On September 3, he started and finished both games of a doubleheader against Milwaukee, winning the first game 10–0, but dropping the nightcap 6–1. Nine days later, he repeated the feat against Philadelphia, again pitching the full two games. He won the first, 4–3, but was beaten in the second, 5–4.

Two years later, Iron Man McGinnity was pitching for the New York Giants in the National League. The 1903 season would see him set a National League mark with 434 innings pitched, while compiling a 31–20 record. But that wasn't the most impressive record he set that year.

On August 1, he once again pitched both games of a doubleheader against Boston. This time he won them both, 4–1 and 5–2. A week later, on August 8, he repeated the performance, defeating Brooklyn 6–1 and 4–3. And on August 31, that same season, he once again hurled a pair, this time against Philadelphia. And for the third time he finished both games a winner, 4–1 and 9–2.

So the Iron Man became the only pitcher in baseball history to pitch and win three complete doubleheaders in one season. He is also the only pitcher to throw five complete doubleheaders in a career, another one of those early baseball records that will undoubtedly stand forever because of the changing game.

Whitey and the Babe— Something in Common

Yankee fans might know this one, but it's tricky. What do Babe Ruth and Whitey Ford have in common? The obvious answer would seem to be that they are both Hall of Fame players who achieved their greatest success with the New York Yankees. True, they do share that honor and distinction. But did you know that Babe Ruth once held a prestigious record that was finally broken by Whitey Ford?

Sounds impossible at first. Ruth, the mighty Bambino, is a man known for his many long home runs and dynamic slugging. Ford, the crafty southpaw, the Yankee ace of the fifties and sixties, is considered by many as the finest Yankee hurler ever. These two share a record? It happened, all right, but it was not a mark set by the Babe when he was a slugger for the Yankees, but when he was a young pitcher with the Boston Red Sox.

For those who might have forgotten, the Babe started out as a pitcher, and he was a fine one at that.

Chances are he would have been a Hall of Fame hurler had he not been able to hit a baseball longer and farther than anyone else. The Red Sox called George Herman Ruth up as a hard-throwing nineteen-year-old in 1914. A year later, at the age of twenty, Ruth fashioned an 18–8 record and was touted as one of the up-and-coming pitching stars in the American League.

He didn't disappoint the following year, going 23–12 for the season and helping to pitch the Red Sox all the way to the World Series. The Sox faced the old Brooklyn Dodgers in the 1916 classic and the Babe got the call in game two. He pitched brilliantly. The Dodgers pushed across a run in the first and after that they couldn't touch the tall lefty.

The problem was the Red Sox couldn't do much, either. They tied the game in the third, then the goose eggs began appearing on the scoreboard. It was knotted after nine and into extra innings. Ruth was still on the mound shutting down the Dodgers, and when the Sox finally scored in the bottom of the fourteenth, they made the Babe a winner.

After giving up a run in the first frame, Babe Ruth had worked 13⅓ straight scoreless innings for the victory. His effort gave the Sox a 2–0 lead in the Series and they went on to win it in five games without having to use the Babe again.

He was 24–13 in 1917 and in 1918 began splitting his time between pitching and the outfield. His home-run bat was beginning to bring fans into the ballpark. So his pitching mark was just 13–7, but he contributed 11 home runs and 64 runs batted in with just 317 at-bats. He was a major factor in yet another Red Sox pennant and trip to the World Series.

This time the Bosox faced the Chicago Cubs, and despite all the time the Babe had spent in the outfield, he was the choice as opening-game pitcher. It was a good choice. Once again the hard-throwing Babe pitched goose eggs, and the Sox shut out the Cubbies, 1–0.

The Sox had a 2–1 lead in games when the Babe got the call again in game four. Once more he began to mow down the Chicago hitters. Boston picked up a pair of runs in the fourth and the Babe held that lead right through the seventh inning. Finally, in the eighth, the Cubs broke through for a pair to tie it. But the Sox got one back in the bottom of the inning, and although he needed relief help in the ninth, the Babe got still another World Series triumph.

When the Red Sox wrapped up the Series in six games, Babe Ruth was not only on another World Champion team, but he had also become a record breaker. His 16⅓ straight scoreless innings before the Cubs scored, coupled with the 13⅓ scoreless frames in the 1916 classic, gave him a total of 29⅔ straight scoreless World Series innings. It was a great record, all right, and a record that would stand for more than forty years.

It also signaled the virtual end of Babe Ruth's pitching career. The following year, 1919, he started his record-breaking hitting career with 29 home runs, while compiling just a 9–5 mound mark. A year later he was blasting 54 home runs for the New York Yankees, his pitching career all but over.

As a pitcher, he wound up with a 94–46 career mark and an outstanding 2.28 earned run average. He also had set a brilliant World Series pitching mark, his 29⅔ consecutive scoreless innings the game's standard for many years.

In a way, it was only fitting that a Yankee would finally chase Ruth's mound mark. For while he set the standard as a member of the Red Sox, the Babe is certainly most readily identified as a Yank. And from the early 1920s to the mid-1960s, the Yankees were baseball's reigning dynasty, winning pennants and World Series as if they were going out of style.

Whitey Ford came along in the midst of still another great Yankee era. He joined the club midway through the 1950 season and compiled a 9–1 mark. Then after losing two years to military service, he rejoined the club and posted an 18–6 record in 1953. From there, he became the Chairman of the Board, a crafty, clutch pitcher who was always at his best when it meant the most.

He wound up winning 236 games and losing just 106 in a career that ran through 1967. And he was always a man the Yanks would count on in the Series. But it was in the 1960 classic against Pittsburgh that the little lefty really caught fire. He started the third game of the Series that year and blanked the Pirates on just four hits, as the Yanks won it easily, 10–0. Then in the sixth game, with New York trailing by a game, he spun a seven-hit whitewash to even the Series at three games apiece. The Yanks won in a laugher, 12–0.

The Bombers were back in the Series the following season with Whitey Ford having his best year ever. He was 25–4 during the regular season and was on the Yankee Stadium hill for the Series opener against Cincinnati. His dominance continued. He baffled the big Cincinnati bats for nine innings, spinning a neat two-hit shutout as the Yanks won, 2–0.

It was only then that some baseball statisticians noticed that Ford had now thrown 27 straight scoreless innings. He was closing in on the record set by the Babe some forty-three years earlier, a record that had been somewhat forgotten over the years. And when Ford returned to the mound in game four, he knew he was close to the mark.

But very little rattled Whitey Ford. He still dominated the hitters with his array of pitches, and by the end of the third inning, he had broken the record. He threw two more shutout innings before leaving the game with a foot injury after fanning one hitter in the sixth. Jim Coates came on to complete the whitewash and the Yanks went on to win the Series in five games.

And Whitey Ford's string was still alive. He had broken the Babe's mark by throwing 32 straight scoreless innings. So when the Yanks returned to the fall classic in '62 against the Giants, it was just a matter of how far the Chairman of the Board could take the mark. Sure enough, Ford was the starting pitcher in game one.

He retired the Giants in the first inning for his thirty-

New York Yankees ace Whitey Ford shown in action against Cincinnati in the 1961 World Series. Ford shut out the Reds in the opener, and in his next appearance broke Babe Ruth's long-standing record for consecutive shutout innings in World Series play.

third straight scoreless frame. But in the second, the bubble finally burst. The Giants pushed across a run after two were out, ending the streak at 33⅔ innings. Still, Ford and the Yanks won the game, 6–2, and were on their way to still another World Series triumph.

Babe Ruth and Whitey Ford, an unlikely duo when it comes to pitching records. But the record they have in common is quite a mark. The Babe held it for forty-three years, and in the more than twenty-five years since Whitey Ford broke it, there have been some very great pitchers in the World Series. But no one has broken the mark.

Relief Is Just a Pitcher Away

There was a time in baseball when pitchers were expected to finish what they started. Unless a hurler injured himself or was completely ineffective, the same man who walked out to the mound in the first was expected to be out there in the ninth. Looking at the record books from the late nineteenth and early twentieth centuries, there are a host of pitchers with an incredible number of starts and an incredible number of innings.

But even through the 1920s and 1930s, relief pitchers were a rare commodity. It was a job nobody wanted. If you were a reliever, that meant you weren't good enough to start, or were just about washed up, or didn't have an arm worthy of throwing nine innings.

Yet somewhere along the line, the idea of having an outstanding relief pitcher began to take hold. After all, what was wrong with having a fresh arm in the game when the going got tough, a guy who could come out of that bullpen when the game was on the line and do the job. It was probably a case of why didn't someone think of this sooner!

In the 1940s, a number of pitchers began to make their livings by coming out of the bullpen. Most notably, there was Joe Page of the Yankees and Hugh Casey of the Dodgers. In fact, the Yanks had a pitcher named Johnny Murphy who earned the nickname "Fireman" in the latter 1930s because of his abilities coming out of the pen.

But it was in the late 1950s and early 1960s that relief pitchers really came into their own. Relievers such as Jim Konstanty of the Phils, Joe Black of the Dodgers, Hoyt Wilhelm of the Giants, Luis Arroyo of the Yanks, all became stars in their own right. Because of them, there were now young pitchers who decided to become relievers rather than starters. The bullpen ace, or "stopper," was not only a very important part of every team, but had a newfound status as a superstar in his own right.

By the 1970s and 1980s all baseball fans recognized names like Rollie Fingers, Sparky Lyle, Bruce Sutter, Goose Gossage, Kent Tekulve, Dan Quisenberry, Jeff Reardon, Jesse Orosco, and Dave Righetti. With all these relief pitchers coming to prominence, it stands to reason that there were new records and record-breaking performances.

For many years, the record for appearances by a pitcher was held by the immortal Cy Young. Young was a starting pitcher in the days when there wasn't much relief, having toiled in the majors from 1890 to 1911. During that time, Young walked to the mound some 906 times, winning 511 ballgames while losing 313.

He was one of those rubber-armed pitchers who rarely needed relief, averaging more than eight innings a game for twenty-two years. Five different years, Young pitched more than 400 innings and he came close to 400 in several others.

"My arm would get weak and tired at times," Young once said, "but never sore, even though I usually worked with just two days rest, and sometimes with just one. And I only needed about a dozen pitches to warm up for a ballgame."

With an arm like that, Cy Young might very well be a candidate for a relief pitcher today, a short man who had to be ready to go almost every day. His record for total mound appearances stood for years, and many thought it would never go. Then the relievers started coming. And the man who broke it began as an unlikely candidate for the simple reason that he didn't make his major league debut until he was nearly twenty-nine years old.

His name was Hoyt Wilhelm, and he was a right-hander who threw a knuckleball, perhaps the one pitch in baseball that puts very little strain on the arm. Sometimes called a flutterball, the knuckler darts and dances, and can be extremely difficult to hit. Wilhelm was a master of the knuckleball and the pitch would sustain him for twenty-one years.

He made 71 appearances as a Giants' rookie in 1952, winning 15 and losing just 3, all in relief, and he remained one of baseball's best firemen during the entire course of his career. By 1968, Wilhelm was pitching for the Chicago White Sox, his fifth team, and was having another fine year. Then, in mid-July, some baseball statisticians noticed that Wilhelm was creeping up on one of baseball's oldest records.

By July 24, Hoyt Wilhelm had tied Cy Young with 906 career appearances. Then, just two days before his forty-fifth birthday, he broke the mark by working the ninth inning for the White Sox against the Oakland A's. Another of baseball's sacred records had fallen.

Hoyt Wilhelm pitched in the majors until 1972, when he was nearly 49 years old, finishing his career with the Los Angeles Dodgers and with 1,070 mound appearances, a record that still stands today. Ironically, another relief pitcher of the same era, Lindy McDaniel, is now second on the all-time appearance list. McDaniel also broke Cy Young's old mark by appearing in 987 major league ballgames.

Then there was Mike Marshall. He wasn't always a reliever, like Wilhelm. In fact, Marshall struggled throughout his career to really find his niche, as he bounced around with nine different big-league clubs over a fourteen-year span. He started, he relieved, often with mediocre results.

During this period, Marshall became more and more interested in the mechanics of pitching. He went back to college and studied kinesiology, which deals with the movement of the human body. Soon, he began applying his own theories to pitching. For instance, instead of resting his arm, Marshall would throw every day, and in 1973 it looked as if his unique approach to pitching was beginning to pay off.

Working in relief for the Montreal Expos, Marshall appeared in 92 ballgames, setting a new major league record of 31 saves. His won-lost record stood at 14–11, and many people were calling him the best relief pitcher in baseball. With his market value at its highest, the Expos traded him to the Los Angeles Dodgers. Before the 1974 season, Marshall told Dodger management that he was willing to work as often as they needed him. The club took him at his word and he didn't disappoint them.

Marshall was a workhorse from start to finish, and in the process he became a record breaker. The Dodgers played the usual 162 games that year, and Mike Marshall pitched in 106 of them, a single-season record that still stands. He also pitched in 208 innings in relief, another major league mark. In addition, he finished 83 of the 106 games in which he appeared.

That wasn't all. From June 18 through July 3, Mike Marshall set still another record by appearing in 13 consecutive ballgames. He won 15, saved another 21, and had a fine, 2.42 earned run average. Then he topped it all off by becoming the first relief pitcher to win the Cy Young Award given to the best pitcher in the league. The honor proved once and for all that relief pitchers were now on an equal footing with the starters.

While Mike Marshall was the perfect example of the workhorse relief pitcher, there are also those who are specialists, used only in specific situations and often facing only a single batter. Darold Knowles, a highly successful reliever in the sixties and seventies, was often used in such a way.

Knowles was a sidearming lefthander, especially adept at getting left-handed batters out. Consequently, Knowles was often used in situations where a particular left-handed batter had to be neutralized. And never was this more in evidence than in the 1973 World Series. Pitching for the Oakland A's, Knowles was called upon in each of the seven games his club played against the New York Mets.

It was a record-breaking performance. Knowles came in as early as the fourth inning in one game, and saved a pair, getting the final outs in the first and seventh games.

And so the parade continues. The 1980s saw more quality relief pitchers and more record-setting performances. There is no longer any doubt that the relief pitcher, especially the stopper, is as important as the 20-game winner to a winning baseball team.

In 1981, Rollie Fingers joined the Milwaukee Brewers after a very successful career with Oakland, and proceeded to turn in still another record-setting performance. Fingers had been the big stopper for Oakland during the A's World Series seasons of 1972, '73, and '74, and he continued to pitch top-flight relief throughout the 1970s. When Fingers first pitched for the Brewers in 1981, he was already thirty-five years old. But there was plenty of life left in his arm.

The 1981 season was shortened by the players' strike, but it couldn't dim Fingers' achievements. He appeared in 47 games, won 6 and saved 28. That meant he played a major role in 34 of the club's 62 victories. His earned run average was an anemic 1.04. But it was after the season that Fingers became a record breaker.

He became the first relief pitcher to be named both the Cy Young Award winner and the Most Valuable Player in the same year. It was quite an achievement, yet a feat that has already been duplicated. In 1984, Detroit's Willie Hernandez turned in the same kind of performance as the stopper, leading the Tigers to the American League pennant and World Series. Like Fingers, Hernandez won both the Cy Young and MVP.

In today's game, then, there seems to be no limit to the heights the relief pitcher can reach. Many of the best ones seem to have some kind of gimmick, or unusual pitch going for them. Kansas City's Dan Quisenberry has a unique, submarine delivery that baffled hitters so much that the "Quiz" was able to set a new mark of 45 saves. Bruce Sutter used the split-fingered fastball to tie that record of 45 saves.

But in 1986, a relief pitcher emerged as a record breaker without any kind of trick pitch or delivery. In fact, had it not been for some kind of fate, this man would not have been a relief pitcher at all.

He's Dave Righetti of the New York Yankees, a six-three, lefthander who, as they say, throws smoke. There's nothing tricky about Rags. Fastball, curve, fastball—old-fashioned power pitching channeled into one or two innings of overwhelming relief. But when Righetti first joined the Bronx Bombers, it was as a nine-inning pitcher.

Rags was Rookie of the Year in '81, and big things

All relief pitchers do it differently. Kansas City's Dan Quisenberry, one of the best of the '80s, uses a submarine delivery that drives hitters crazy. The "Quiz" held the record of 45 saves until it was broken by Dave Righetti in 1986.

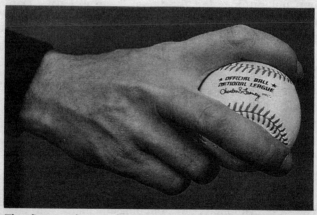

The fingers that made the split-fingered fastball famous. Relief pitcher Bruce Sutter demonstrates the grip that gave his fastball that sudden, sharp dip. The same grip is used by other split-finger proponents, such as Houston's Mike Scott.

were predicted for him. He seemed a sure 20-game winner. So he continued as a starter with the Yanks, and on July 4, 1983, showed what he could do when he had his best stuff. That day, Dave Righetti took to the mound and tossed a no-hitter, the first by a Yankee since Don Larsen's perfect game in the 1956 World Series. He was 14–8 as a starter that year and seemed on the brink of a big season.

But in the offseason, the Yanks learned that their bullpen ace, Rich "Goose" Gossage, wouldn't be back. Suddenly, they were a team without a stopper. Instead of making a trade, they looked from within. They asked Dave Righetti to make the move to the bullpen.

It was a lot to ask of a youngster who seemed to have a limitless future as a starter. But Rags thought it over and decided to give it a try.

"I was green and had to really feel my way through it," Righetti said. "I didn't even know how to warm up."

There were adjustments, and Yankee pitching coach Mark Connor explained a few of them.

"He had to get used to everyday throwing," Connor said, "and being involved with more than half the team's games. But I think the biggest adjustment was that as the stopper he might have to pitch five days in a row."

But Rags made the adjustment. He had 31 saves in 1984, 29 the next year. Then came 1986. Though there had been talk about returning him to the starting rotation from time to time, it was beginning to look as if he was in the bullpen to stay.

41

"I still say that a starting pitcher is more popular, because there's more glamour as a starter," he said, "but being a reliever in New York is also a top position."

Rags started well in 1986, but when he encountered a midyear slump, there was more talk about returning him to the starting rotation. The slump reached a climax in Toronto in late June. Rags came in to protect a six-run Yankee lead in the ninth. Suddenly, the Blue Jays erupted for six runs, with George Bell blasting a grand slammer to tie the game. As Manager Lou Piniella walked slowly to the mound, Rags took a new ball and suddenly heaved it clear over the rightfield fence. That's the frustration of being a stopper and not stopping.

"A reliever has to learn to take more setbacks," Rags said. "I've gotten better, but I'm still a lousy loser."

But the game in Toronto was a turning point. Shortly thereafter, Dave Righetti became the best reliever in baseball. He caught fire, making good on 29 of his final 30 save opportunities, and along the way he became a record breaker.

In the final months, he was racking up save after save. And even though the Yanks wouldn't catch the front-running Boston Red Sox, Rags was helping them solidify their hold on second. Then in a doubleheader on October 4, in Boston, the big lefty came on to save both games. They meant nothing to the pennant race, but plenty to Dave Righetti.

The stopper. That was the Yankees' Dave Righetti in 1986 when he set a major league record with 46 saves. Once a promising starting pitcher, "Rags" made the switch to the bullpen and became a superstar.

For the two saves gave him 46 on the season, breaking the record held jointly by Sutter and Quisenberry. It was quite a year, and it showed once again the impact a top-flight relief pitcher can have on his team.

With his 46 saves and 8 victories, Dave Righetti contributed to 60 percent of the Yanks' 90 victories. Even more amazing was the fact that the team had a 60–14 record in games in which Rags appeared. That's an .811 winning percentage.

Relief pitchers. They've come a long way, and in a changing game, they are definitely here to stay.

And Now for Some One-Shots

In the middle 1960s, the Milwaukee Braves had a young pitcher named Tony Cloninger. In his fourth year in the league, 1964, Cloninger won 19 and lost 14. A year later Cloninger went 24–11 and looked to be one of the coming mound stars of the National League.

He never quite fulfilled his promise, but before he left the game after the 1972 season, Tony Cloninger set a National League record that still stands. But, surprisingly, it wasn't a pitching mark. No, Tony Cloninger set his record with his bat.

Cloninger was the starting pitcher in a July 3, 1966, game in San Francisco. The Braves had moved from Milwaukee to Atlanta then, and Cloninger wasn't doing as well as he had the two previous years. So he was concerned about his pitching. But on this day, the Braves really had their hitting shoes on, and Cloninger got to bat in the first inning with the bases loaded.

Facing the Giants' Bob Priddy, Cloninger took a big rip and connected. The ball sailed over the wall for a grand-slam home run. A smiling Cloninger circled the bases. After all, how often does a pitcher hit a home run, let alone a grand slam. Staked to a big lead, he relaxed and began to concentrate on his pitching.

When he came to bat again, it was the fourth inning and this time he was facing relief pitcher Ray Sadecki. But one thing hadn't changed. Once again the Braves had the bases full. Sadecki fired his fastball and Cloninger swung from the heels. Whack!

He had hit another shot. It sailed high and deep . . . and over the fence! Tony Cloninger had hit his second grand slam, setting a record as the only National Leaguer in history to hit two grand slams in one game. Later, he had a run-scoring single for a total of nine RBIs in a 17–3 victory.

Never has a pitcher put on such a hitting show. But the record he set wasn't for pitchers. It was for everyone. And yet a pitcher did it, and supposedly a weak-hitting pitcher. Which just goes to prove that you never know in baseball.

Every pitcher dreams of throwing a no-hitter. Sometimes, those dreams can turn into a nightmare. For instance, two out, ninth inning, one more out for a no-hit ballgame and . . . base hit! It's happened. But there have also been many no-hitters, and in a few rare cases, that gem of gems, a perfect game.

Then there are the multiple no-hitters, pitchers who have thrown at least a pair. Sandy Koufax, the former Dodger great, had four, while Nolan Ryan, still pitching for the Astros in the mid 1980s, is the record breaker with five no-hit ballgames.

And five modern-day pitchers—Koufax, Catfish Hunter, Jim Bunning, Len Barker and Mike Witt—have put their names in the books with perfect games. So every pitcher dreams of the day he can leave the mound after nine innings and see all zeroes, goose eggs, on the scoreboard.

But there was one pitcher who not only dreamed the dream, but also lived it in a way no other no-hit pitcher ever has, before or since. His name was Johnny Vander Meer, and he pitched in the big leagues from 1937 to 1951, missing two seasons during World War II.

Vander Meer had a number of solid seasons in the Bigs, his best being an 18–12 log in 1942. But when all was said and done, he was basically a .500 pitcher, finishing his career at 119–121. Yet in 1938, his second year with the Cincinnati Reds, Johnny Vander Meer set a record that has never been matched.

The lefty was putting together a pretty fair year when he took the mound for a June 11 start against Boston at Cincinnati's Crosley Field. Early in the game it became obvious that Vander Meer had his good stuff. He was setting the Braves down without any problem.

Boston's Danny MacFayden also pitched well, matching Vandy for three innings. But Cincy pushed across a run in the fourth, then got two more in the sixth when catcher Ernie Lombardi blasted a homer with a man aboard. The way Vander Meer was pitching, the 3–0 lead looked solid enough.

By the seventh inning Vander Meer's teammates stopped talking to him. It was the old baseball superstition. You don't say anything to a pitcher who's throwing a no-hitter, and that's what the lefty was doing. Sure enough, Vander Meer completed his gem, shutting out the Braves on nothing more than three walks.

The dream come true. Like all no-hit pitchers, Vander Meer couldn't have been happier. For a twenty-three-year-old, this was the ultimate. No one could have blamed Vandy if he let down in his next start four days later at Brooklyn.

This one was special in a lot of ways. For one thing, it was the first official major league night game ever played at old Ebbets Field. So you could say that the lights were a factor, but then again, they didn't bother the Cincinnati hitters. Anyway, a capacity crowd was on hand for the game and Vander Meer started off the same way he had finished four days earlier. He wasn't giving up a hit.

The Reds jumped on the Dodgers for four runs in the third, and would get two more before the night ended. But the big story was Vander Meer. After three innings, four innings, five innings, six innings, he still hadn't given up a hit. Everyone knew what was happening, and everyone knew it hadn't happened before. Could Johnny Vander Meer pitch a second consecutive no-hitter?

With the pressure on, the youngster bore down. Sure enough, he worked through the last three innings without yielding a single hit. And when he got the final out, bedlam broke loose. Johnny Vander Meer had become the first and only pitcher in big league history to throw back-to-back no-hitters.

Not only did Johnny Vander Meer pitch himself into the record books, his achievement assured his immortality. Because every time a pitcher throws a no-hit game, someone will begin wondering about his next start, and whether he will do it again. They'll wonder if he'll be able to duplicate that incredible record-breaking performance of Johnny Vander Meer.

The magical thing about a no-hit game is that it puts its author on center stage, if only for a short time. Johnny Vander Meer will be remembered forever, though he was an average pitcher, at best. Nolan Ryan and Sandy Koufax, who pitched multiple no-hitters, will be remembered for their total pitching achievements. And then there are those pitchers who have a no-hitter as their *only* claim to fame.

Back in 1953, the St. Louis Browns had a twenty-eight-year-old rookie pitcher named Alva Lee "Bobo" Holloman, from Thomaston, Georgia. The Browns had a lot of new players coming and going in those days, because they were always looking for ways to climb out of the area of the American League basement.

So Holloman didn't create any particular stir when the Browns kept him on their roster at the outset of the '53 season. Yet within a month, he would pitch himself into the major league record books . . . and two months after that he'd be gone!

In April, the Browns used Holloman sparingly. He made just four relief appearances and really didn't distinguish himself. Then, on May 6, he was penciled in for his first big-league start. He'd be facing the old Philadelphia A's in a night game at St. Louis. To the surprise of everyone, Holloman began mowing down the A's and looking like a world beater in the process.

The usually punchless Browns would score six runs on that cool May evening, and one of the hitting stars was also Bobo Holloman. He had a pair of hits and knocked in three of the six runs. But his pitching was still the big story. Going into the final innings, Bobo Holloman hadn't given up a base hit.

Sure enough, Holloman completed his no-hitter. The only A's to reach base did so on five walks. And a quick check of the record books confirmed something else. Bobo Holloman had set a major league record by becoming the only pitcher in baseball history to throw a no-hitter in his first big league start.

Was this a preview of things to come? Did the St. Louis Browns have themselves a new mound sensation? Sorry, but it didn't work out that way. With visions of the no-hitter still dancing in his head, Bobo Holloman was only able to win two more games. On July 23, he had just a 3–7 record and the Browns suddenly sold his contract to Toronto of the International League.

So just two and a half months from perhaps the greatest achievement of his life, Bobo Holloman was back in the minor leagues. He tried to work his way to the majors again, but couldn't. Before long, he was out of baseball, saying good-bye to a big-league career that lasted barely four months.

Yet because of one game, one big moment when everything went just right, Alva Lee Holloman pitched himself into the record books.

The Triple Crown. Special words to a baseball fan. It's an achievement not to be taken lightly. For a player who wins the triple crown is a player who has just put together an absolutely super season. He will have led the league in all three major hitting categories: batting average, home runs, and runs batted in.

So for openers, it takes a slugger to win the triple crown, because he's got to be able to lead the league in home runs. But he can't be the kind of slugger who swings for the fences every time up. That's because he also must get enough other hits to lead the league in hitting. And to top that off, he has to have the kind of year and the kind of team that will enable him to drive home more runs than any of the other big hitters in the league. So it's obviously not an easy bill to fill.

Only a handful of major leaguers have won the triple crown, and it seems to be harder than ever to achieve. Many of today's sluggers just don't have the kind of batting average necessary to have a shot. And the list of players who *never* won the triple crown reads like a Who's Who in the Hall of Fame.

Some of the great players who never won it include Babe Ruth, Joe DiMaggio, Willie Mays, Henry Aaron,

Reggie Jackson, Stan Musial, Johnny Bench, Mike Schmidt, George Brett, and Don Mattingly. In fact, no one has won it since Carl Yastrzemski of the Red Sox did it in 1967. Of today's players, the Yankees' Mattingly would seem to have the best chance. He's already won the batting title and has led the league in RBIs. He's also hit 35 homers one year. So with the dandy first baseman, it's a possibility.

The first triple crown winner was the great Ty Cobb way back in 1909. That was the era of the dead ball, so Cobb did it by leading the American League with just nine homers and 115 RBIs. Three years later, Heinie Zimmerman of the Chicago Cubs did it with 14 homers and just 98 ribbies, though both Cobb and Zimmerman batted in the .370s.

But once the lively ball came in, the triple crown winners put up some impressive numbers. The great Lou Gehrig won it in 1934 with a .363 batting average, 49 homers, and 165 RBIs. Those are numbers, all right. Other triple crown winners include the likes of Chuck Klein, Jimmie Foxx, Joe Medwick, Mickey Mantle, and Frank Robinson. Not a bad group.

There are two players that were purposely left out of the above list. That's because they're the record breakers, the only players in baseball history to have won the coveted triple crown twice. Both are among baseball's all-time greats. They are Roger Hornsby in the National League and Ted Williams in the American.

Hornsby turned the trick in 1922 and 1925. The first time he did it with an amazing .401 batting average, 42 home runs, and 152 runs batted in. Three years later, he hit a blazing .403, smacked 39 round-trippers, and drove home 143 runs. Incredible numbers for one of the finest hitters who ever lived.

Ted Williams showed he had triple crown potential in his rookie season of 1939. As a twenty-one-year-old, he batted .327, had 31 homers, and led the league with 145 RBIs. Two years later he batted .406, becoming baseball's last .400 hitter, and a year after that, in 1942, he won his first triple crown.

That year Ted batted .356, slammed 36 home runs, and drove home 137 runs. It was still another great season. But then Ted lost three prime years to military service, flying combat missions in World War II. His second year back from the war, 1947, he tied Hornsby's record by winning the triple once more.

He batted .343 that year, connected for 32 homers and 114 RBIs. It wasn't even his greatest year, but it was good enough to put him in the record books alongside the Rajah.

To Catch a Thief

They're exciting. They disrupt. They put on pressure. They ignite. They cause mistakes. And they win ballgames . . . or perhaps it is more accurate to say they steal ballgames. They're baseball's thieves, the base stealers, the guys with the flashing feet. Because they're always a threat to run, they can wage psychological warfare with the pitcher and catcher. Base stealers are an offensive weapon as old as the game itself, and there are times when they're every bit as important as the home-run sluggers.

Base stealing was an integral part of early baseball, before the turn of the century. Though the rules were different, there were still daring men flying around the basepaths. A player named Harry Stovey set the all-time record before 1900 by swiping 156 bases back in 1888. Three years later "Slidin'" Billy Hamilton pilfered 115. Hamilton also stole 937 sacks during his career.

When the modern-day rules came in after 1900, the stolen base was still a big part of the game. Great players such as Ty Cobb, Honus Wagner, Eddie Collins, Max Carey, George Sisler, Sam Rice, and Frankie Frisch all made the stolen base a real offensive weapon.

Then in the 1930s, the steal began to take a backseat to power. Babe Ruth and his mammoth home runs helped change the face of the game, and the stolen base was not the strategical force it had always been before. It stayed that way right into the middle 1950s. Then the steal began to re-emerge. Two players were mainly responsible. Both were shortstops. They were Luis Aparicio of Chicago in the American League and Maury Wills of the Dodgers in the National.

Others followed. Speed once again became an important part of the game, a weapon, and it's stayed that way right up to today, with one great base stealer following another. And with the emphasis on the stolen base once again, the records have fallen. Let's take a look at some of these daring record breakers.

The first record-breaking base stealer after 1900 was none other than Tyrus Raymond Cobb, the Georgia Peach, and a man still considered by many to be the greatest ever to play the game. When he retired, Cobb left a host of records behind, a number of which still stand today, such as his .367 lifetime batting average, and 12 American League batting titles, 9 of which came in succession.

Some of his other marks have been bettered, but no one can ever wipe out the image Ty left behind when he retired in 1928. He was perhaps baseball's greatest competitor, a man who played each and every game as if it was war. Cobb never gave an inch and as a result wasn't always the most popular player on the diamond. But, oh, was he ever effective.

Needless to say, the speedy Cobb was the premier base stealer of his day, the man who set the standards for those who followed. It was Ty Cobb who said "the game of baseball is an unrelenting war of nerves," and whenever he was on the bases he tried to prove it. He was always a threat to go, and whenever he was challenged, he'd answer. There were always stories (though no evidence) that Cobb sharpened his spikes and was willing to use them when someone got in his way. Cobb wouldn't have denied this, because he pressed for every advantage, no matter how small.

There were a host of outstanding base stealers in Ty's day, but he led the league six times. In 1915, the Georgia Peach set a standard that everyone would aim at for years. He swiped 96 that season, and was so consistently outstanding during his long career that he finished with another record. Some felt his 892 career steals would stand forever.

Cobb was a big man for his day, standing six-one, and weighing in the neighborhood of 190 pounds. Yet he was fast, and if he came straight into the bag, the fielder knew he could be in for a jolt. Cobb knew how to take advantage of this. If the fielder braced himself for Ty coming straight in, he might use a hook slide, falling away and catching the corner of the bag with his toe. He also used the fall-away slide, where he would sweep wide with his entire body and reach back with his arm to catch the corner.

That was Cobb. The opposition never knew what he would do next. Even when his body was bruised and battered from sliding on the old, rough infields of his day, he'd go all out, never letting up even for an instant. And he'd look for the edge, always the edge. One time, a sportswriter mentioned that he noticed Ty had a nervous habit of kicking the first-base bag a few times whenever he reached. Cobb just laughed.

"It wasn't a nervous habit," he said. "That's just what I wanted everyone to think. It was really a percentage trick. I took a long lead and pitchers were always trying to pick me off. So I needed every advantage. I didn't just kick the bag. I always kicked it a couple of inches closer to second base. That way, I'd have an extra edge when I had to get back fast and the pickoff throw was close."

And Cobb studied the opposition, leaving no stone unturned. One day St. Louis catcher Lou Criger boasted that he'd gun Ty down like a dead pigeon if the Peach tried to run on him. All Ty did that day was steal five bases. And one time he told Criger he was going, then stole second, third, and home. When asked how he did it, Ty said it had nothing to do with Criger or his throwing arm.

"I knew the pitcher that day, knew him well. I could have run on him anytime and made it."

That was Ty Cobb, ballplayer and baserunner extraordinaire. He set the standard and challenged the others to come.

By the middle 1950s, Ty Cobb still held the single-season and career base-stealing records. But there were signs that speed was coming back. In 1956, the great Willie Mays, a super all-around player, swiped 40 bases for the New York Giants. It was the most steals in the National League since 1929. Three years later, in 1959, Luis Aparicio of the White Sox won his fourth straight American League base-stealing title. He had a career high 56 thefts that year (he would later steal 57), the most in the junior circuit since 1943 and before that 1931.

Then in 1960, shortstop Maury Wills of the Dodgers won his first base-stealing title with 50 thefts. Two years later, Wills would write headlines with his der-ring-do on the basepaths, becoming a record breaker in the process and putting the stolen base back on the baseball map for keeps.

Wills was twenty-nine years old in 1962, yet only in his fourth season in the majors. He wasn't a big man, standing 5'11" and weighing just 170 pounds. And while he had excellent speed, he wasn't what would be called a blazer. Yet he played the game with the same intensity as Cobb, and was a fiery competitor.

The Dodger teams in those years didn't have a whole lot of power. They depended more on pitching, defense, and speed, and Maury Wills realized his base stealing could be a real catalyst. So when 1962 rolled around, he began to really pour it on. From the outset of the season he started stealing bases at a pace that rivaled Cobb's.

There hadn't been a real assault on Cobb's mark of 96 steals since he set it nearly a half century earlier. So it wasn't surprising that Maury Wills' flying feet grabbed the attention of the baseball world. The fact that the Dodgers were in a hot divisional race with the Giants didn't hurt, either.

Hitting around the .300 mark most of the year, and getting the at-bats from his leadoff position, Wills spent a lot of time on base and made the most of it. When the season ended he had set a new standard, stealing 104 bases and breaking one of the oldest marks in the book. It was an exhausting season for Wills, but he truly thought the record he had set would stand for a long time.

"I didn't think anyone would approach it for years," Wills admitted, "maybe not even in my lifetime."

It wasn't an easy record for Wills to break. The constant hook sliding took a toll on his body, perhaps best evidenced by his falling off to just 40 steals the next season. But he was no flash in the pan. In 1965, Wills had another big year with 94 thefts. Again, the pounding took its toll as he slipped to 38 in '66.

But he had shown that the steal could again be a formidable weapon and the lesson wasn't lost, especially on a young player named Lou Brock.

Brock was a Chicago Cubs rookie in 1962, the same year Wills set the new record. But he admitted that he came into the game with something other than stolen bases on his mind.

"There was so much emphasis on the home run then," he said, "and that's where I thought the money was."

Brock had plenty to learn. He stole just 16 bases his

rookie year, and they came by way of natural ability. The next year he had 24 steals, but he wasn't improving. His batting average was around .250 and he was not a good outfielder. When things stayed about the same by June of 1964, he suddenly found himself traded to the St. Louis Cardinals.

The Cards were on the way to a pennant that year, and suddenly Lou Brock woke up. After moving to St. Louis in June, he changed his style, hitting .348 for the rest of the year (.315 combined with his Chicago average) and winding up with 43 steals. Of that number, 33 came after the midyear trade.

St. Louis won the World Series from the Yanks that year and Lou Brock had become an established star. He would play the remainder of his career at a Hall of Fame level, winding up with more than 3,000 hits. And he would also become a record breaker on the basepaths.

The next two years his steals went to 63 and then 74. He was working hard at his craft now, perfecting it, and in doing so was becoming the most consistent base stealer of his time. And he did things in a different way than either Cobb or Wills.

For one thing, Lou used the same technique each time he ran. No tricks; no fancy slides. Nothing unexpected. And he decided on this method after watching the beating Maury Wills took using his hook slides.

"It's a beautiful, but damaging slide," Brock said, "because a larger portion of your body—legs, rump, arms, elbows, and even your back—can make contact

Safe again! Lou Brock swipes yet another base, one of a record 938 he pilfered during his career. Brock also set a mark of 118 thefts in a single season, only to see it broken by Oakland's Rickey Henderson, who upped the standard to 130.

with the ground. I decided to use the straight-in, or pop-up slide. That way, just my calves absorb any real contact or punishment."

Brock also became an acute student of pitchers, studying the moves and mannerisms of each one. Once he learned to "read" the different pitchers, stealing bases became much easier.

"By reading the pitcher the baserunner knows when to run and when he can get his best jump," he explained. "And it's all related to leading. The amount of lead a runner takes is related to confidence and ability to read the pitcher. Then a runner must practice and improve upon his initial thrust. He's got to be able to move out and be at maximum speed within ten steps or so."

These are things that some very fast runners cannot do. So even with all their speed, they will never be great base stealers. But the five-eleven, 170-pound Brock was proving a very great base stealer. He was an important cog in the Cardinals' attack, a superstar who helped them win pennants in 1967 and '68, and a player who rose to the occasion, playing brilliantly in both World Series.

During this time he continued to steal over 50 bases a year, with a high of 74 in 1966. By 1974, Brock was nearly thirty-five years old, approaching the twilight of his career. He had swiped 70 bases in 1973, so he didn't seem to be slowing down. In fact, many felt he had a shot at Cobb's all-time mark of 892. But no one was prepared for what Lou Brock did in 1974.

He began stealing early and often, acting more like a twenty-one-year-old than a ballplayer nearly thirty-five. By the time his club had played 56 games, Brock had 40 steals. It was beginning to look as if he had a shot at Wills' single-season mark. And even Wills himself admitted it was tougher in '74 than it had been in '62.

"When I broke Cobb's mark," Wills said, "everyone was home-run conscious, and the pitchers weren't used to keeping runners close to first. But after I stole

104, the game kind of changed. Pitchers started working on keeping the good baserunners close to first and not letting them get a huge jump."

And Brock said the catchers were also quicker. With more base stealers, the young backstops all threw well and welcomed the challenge of cutting down the top runners. But Brock continued to swipe bases. By the time the team reached the halfway mark, Brock had 50 steals. But when the number was at 66 on August 1, some thought he was slowing down, that age was taking its toll.

Then in a weekend series with the Phils, Lou ran wild. He stole eight bases in nine tries, giving him 74 steals in 109 games. When he reached 90 in 130 games, he had the record well within reach. Despite his thirty-five years, he was getting stronger as the year passed, not even wilting in the dog days of August.

He got steal number 100 against the Mets on September 6, then four days later against the Phils, he tied and then broke Wills' record. Baseball had a new stolen-base king, a new record breaker.

"I always felt it was my record," said the candid Wills. "I don't think anyone looks forward to seeing his record broken. So, honestly, I was hoping he wouldn't do it, but once he got around 80, it became very obvious. My hat's off to him."

With several weeks still remaining, Brock extended the record even further, finishing the season with a new mark of 118 stolen bases. For a thirty-five-year-old athlete, it was simply amazing. And Brock wasn't finished. He continued to play and steal bases, cracking Cobb's lifetime mark and becoming the first player to top the 900-steal barrier. He finished his great career with 938 steals, and the question arose immediately, would there be a player to top Lou Brock?

But the game was changing. The young players coming out of the colleges and the minor leagues saw what Lou Brock had done, saw what a weapon the stolen base could be. In addition, coaches and managers knew the game of the eighties was speed, especially since so many new stadiums have artificial turf. Playing on the carpet, the ball moves quickly, so the players must move quickly, too.

So some of the young players were ready as soon as they reached the majors. Midway through the 1979 season the Oakland A's brought up a twenty-year-old outfielder from Ogden named Rickey Henderson. At five-ten, 195-pounds, Henderson didn't have the build of the sleek sprinter. But he could run, and he could steal.

In just 89 games that first year, he swiped 33 bases. A year later, he was making a run at Lou Brock's record. His powerful legs enabled him to get that initial thrust Brock had spoken about. And instead of a hook, fallaway, or pop-up slide, Henderson went in headfirst. He figured he got to the base faster that way.

Though he fell just short of Wills and Brock, young Rickey Henderson became just the third man in baseball history to swipe 100 bases, finishing right at that magic number. It enabled him to set an American

League record, and at the age of twenty-one, most people felt he was the man to break them all.

The next year he was limited to just 108 games by the players' strike. Yet he still swiped 56 sacks, and when 1982 rolled around, he was ready to run. From opening day he was a demon on the basepaths, and the stolen bases came in droves. He was way ahead of Brock's pace, and before the season was half over, it was obvious that only an injury could prevent Rickey Henderson from becoming the new single-season stolen-base champ.

Unlike Wills and Brock, Henderson didn't use the scientific approach to stealing. He just ran.

"I didn't really know a lot about reading pitchers that year," he said, several years later. "I just went on instinct. I think I'm a better base stealer now than when I was just a runner."

But his instincts must have been awfully good. Though he missed some 13 games due to injury in 1982, Rickey Henderson wiped out Lou Brock's record by stealing 130 sacks. It was an incredible performance. And at his age, he had a long way to go.

A year later, he set another pair of stolen-base marks. His 108 thefts made him the first man in baseball history to record back-to-back, 100-steal seasons, and he was also the first to steal 100 or more bases in three different seasons. In 1984, Rickey "slumped" to just 66 steals. But a year later, traded to the New York Yankees, he swiped 80 sacks, and followed it up with 87 in 1986.

Unlike the other stolen-base record breakers, Ty Cobb, Maury Wills and Lou Brock, Rickey Henderson prefers to go into a base head first. Here the Oakland A's star shows his technique en route to a record-breaking 130 steals in 1982. Henderson was later traded to the Yankees and continued to steal at a record-setting clip.

During those two years, he became an even stronger hitter, slamming 24 and 28 home runs respectively, becoming the only American Leaguer in history to hit more than 20 homers and steal more than 50 bases in the same season. And he's already done it twice.

Ricky Henderson is considered one of baseball's superstars, but he won't rest on his laurels. He wants to get better and he wants to keep stealing bases.

"It's important to me to stay on top as a base stealer," he said. "I started out leading the league and I want to finish that way. The only way it won't happen is if I'm slowing down and they get somebody with a jet."

At the end of the 1987 season, Rickey had over 700 stolen bases. His next goal is to surpass Lou Brock's

938 to become the career leader. At his age and at his pace, it's a goal that should be very reachable in the next few years. Of course, in today's game, if Rickey Henderson should slow down, there's already someone waiting to take his place.

The next base-stealing superstar could very well be Vince Coleman of the St. Louis Cardinals. Coleman burst on the scene in 1985 as a rookie with blazing speed and the ability to steal. And it didn't take him long to become a record breaker. As a rookie he swiped 110 bases, a new mark for first-year players, and for a while it looked as if he might challenge Henderson.

Proving it was no fluke, Coleman pilfered 107 sacks his sophomore year, becoming the first player ever to steal 100 or more bases in each of his first two seasons, then followed with 108 in 1987. Another record. His future seems limitless.

So they keep coming. Cobb, Wills, Brock, Henderson, Coleman. There's always someone else, always someone to break the records. Why do they do it? Perhaps something Lou Brock said some years ago best captures the essence of the men who steal bases.

"First base is nowhere," Brock said, "and most times it's useless to stay there. On the other hand, second base is probably the safest place on the field. When I steal second, I practically eliminate the doubleplay, and I can score on almost anything hit past the infield."

And so they continue to run.

Matty's Triple Masterpiece

This one goes back a long way. It was an amazing record then, and it's an amazing record now. More than eighty years have passed since the immortal Christy Mathewson pitched his way into the record books. Why go back now? For one thing, it's always interesting to revisit some of the early greats of the game to see how they performed. And secondly, there have been several other outstanding pitchers who have come close to the record, very close, but just not quite close enough.

Christy Mathewson was the idol of his day, a big, handsome man, soft-spoken and articulate, one of the few players of that time who came out of college. He joined the New York Giants at the turn of the century, in 1900, and within three years was one of the best pitchers in baseball. He won 30 or more games four times, three of them coming in succession, and was a 20-game or better winner for 12 consecutive seasons.

Matty, as he was called, was a real artist on the mound. Standing nearly six feet, two inches tall and weighing 195 pounds, he was one of the bigger players of his day, and he was a real artist to watch. He had a smooth delivery and impeccable control, as well as a trick pitch that often got him out of trouble. In Matty's era they called it the fadeaway. Today, it's better known as the screwball.

When he called it quits after the 1916 season, Christy Mathewson had won 373 ballgames and lost just 188. He and Grover Cleveland Alexander hold the record for most wins ever by a National League pitcher. But perhaps the record for which Christy Mathewson is best remembered was the one he set in the World Series of 1905.

He had been great all year, pitching the Giants to the pennant with a 31–8 record and nine shutouts. In the process he led the league with 206 strikeouts and walked just 64. But the World Series wouldn't be easy, as John McGraw's New Yorkers would be going up against Connie Mack's Philadelphia A's.

It was expected to be a pitchers' series. Besides Matty, the Giants had Joe "Iron Man" McGinnity, who had won 21 games and would start when Matty didn't. But the A's were loaded with arms, too. The duo of Rube Waddell and Eddie Plank had won 27 and 26 games respectively, while Chief Bender chipped in with 16 victories. But shortly before the series began, Waddell injured a shoulder in some horseplay with a teammate. He wouldn't be able to pitch, and his anticipated confrontations with Matty didn't happen.

So it was Mathewson against Plank in the opening game, and the big guy had his good stuff. He gave up just four hits in shutting out the A's 3–0, giving the Giants the opening-game edge. But Chief Bender evened things up in game two, equaling Matty's four-hitter with a 3–0 victory over McGinnity.

Game three saw Matty return to the hill with just three days' rest, this time opposing Andy Coakley of the A's. The results were nearly identical to game one. Matty spun his second straight four-hit shutout, only this time the Giants made it easy by scoring nine runs. They now had a 2–1 lead and Christy Mathewson had a pair of shutouts.

The next was a beauty. When it ended, Iron Man McGinnity had bested Eddie Plank, 1–0, putting the Giants in the driver's seat with a 3–1 edge in games. Manager McGraw then surprised everyone by sending Mathewson back to the hill for game five, this time on only two days' rest. With a 3–1 lead, the manager surely could have rested his ace for another day. But he probably wanted to go for all the marbles right away.

It proved to be the right move. Mathewson was every bit as good as he had been in the two previous games, as he pitched the Giants to a World Series victory and himself into the record book by shutting out the A's for a third time, 2–0. In the third shutout, he yielded just six hits.

Christy Mathewson was the talk of the baseball world, circa 1905. He had set a record by pitching three complete-game shutouts in a single World Series. In fact, all five games resulted in shutouts and the three runs McGinnity had yielded in game two were unearned. So the Giants' staff had a combined earned run average of 0.00.

But the big news was Matty. In three games he gave up a total of 14 hits, struck out 18, and walked just one. It was a performance many people said would never be duplicated. And you know what? They were right. There were, however, a couple of pitchers who came awfully close.

It took a half century for a pitcher to put on a World Series show that would bring back memories of Matty. The year was 1957 and the always-powerful New York Yankees were going up against the surprising Milwaukee Braves. It was a power-laden Yankee team, which boasted the likes of Mickey Mantle, Yogi Berra, Moose Skowron, Elston Howard, Hank Bauer, Enos Slaughter, and Joe Collins. It was doubtful that any pitcher could hold down that lineup for long.

But the Braves had a great one in Warren Spahn, who had won 21 games that year at the age of thirty-six. Their number-two hurler was thirty-year-old Lew Burdette, who had a 17–9 record in '57. Burdette was a fine pitcher. Perhaps his biggest claim to fame, however, entering the 1957 World Series, might have been that he was often suspected of throwing an illegal spitball.

As expected, Spahn got the call in the opener and was matched against Yankee ace Whitey Ford. When Ford and the Bombers came away with a 3–1 victory, the New Yorkers seemed off to a very big advantage.

After all, their best had just beaten Milwaukee's best. So game two became an important one, with Lew Burdette getting the call against Yankee lefty Bobby Shantz.

It started as if it was going to be a hitters' day. The Braves got a run in the top of the second; the Yanks got it back. Milwaukee scored another in the top of the third; the Yanks got it back. So it was 2–2 after three, with neither pitcher looking super sharp. Then in the top of the fourth, the Braves got rid of Shantz by scoring another pair, making it 4–2 after just three and a half innings.

Out came Burdette again. He had given up single runs in the second and third, so the Yankee hitters felt confident. No one could possibly know it then, but Lew Burdette was about to evoke memories of Christy Mathewson. He retired the Yanks without further damage in the fourth. Maybe he was settling down. After a scoreless fifth and sixth, it was apparent he was. His herky-jerky motion and variety of curves and sliders had the Yankee hitters baffled and off balance.

For the rest of the game it was all Burdette. Milwaukee won it, 4–2, and evened the series at a game apiece. But why should one game evoke memories of Mathewson, especially when Burdette gave up a pair of runs and Mathewson gave up nothing? Simple. That pair of runs—one in the second and one in the third— were the only runs Lew Burdette would give up in the Series.

The Yanks won the third game, 12–3, and Milwaukee

came back to take the fourth in 10 innings. Then, it was time for Burdette to get the ball again. This time he'd be facing Whitey Ford in the pivotal fifth game.

It was a classic pitchers' battle all the way, each hurler on top and in command. Still a scoreless game in the bottom of the sixth, the Braves got something going. With two out, Eddie Mathews beat out an infield hit. Then Henry Aaron blooped a single to short right, and big Joe Adcock followed with a sharp hit to right, scoring Mathews.

Just like that the Braves had a run, and it was all they needed. Burdette cruised home with a magnificent seven-hit shutout to give his team a 3–2 lead. But the Yanks were a seasoned World Series team and they bounced right back in game six, winning behind Bullet Bob Turley, 3–2. Now it would come down to a seventh and deciding game.

Warren Spahn was due to be the Milwaukee pitcher. And in spite of Lew Burdette's heroics, the Braves were probably glad their longtime ace was ready for the finale, the biggest game in the history of the franchise, since the Braves had moved to Milwaukee from Boston just a few years earlier.

But the day before the final game, Warren Spahn was knocked out of the box by the flu. Manager Fred Haney had to make a decision, and once again he tabbed Lew Burdette as his starting pitcher. The problem was that Burdette would be pitching with just two days' rest. It seemed unlikely that the fidgety right-hander could have his good stuff for a third time.

Don Larsen, who had pitched the only perfect game in World Series history the year before, was the Yanks' starter. Now, he had another chance to be a hero. It was scoreless for two innings, and the huge Yankee Stadium crowd screamed for the Bombers to put Burdette away. But in the top of the third it was Larsen who was sent to the showers. The Braves erupted for four big runs, and that would be all they needed. They did add an insurance tally in the eighth.

The rest of the day belonged to Lew Burdette. He was every bit as tough as he had been in the previous game, spinning yet another seven-hit shutout. The Braves won the game, 5–0, and were World Champions. And Lew Burdette had come closer than anyone to matching the flawless pitching performance of Christy Mathewson.

Like Matty, Burdette had pitched and won three games, going the distance in each one. And had it not been for the Yanks getting single runs in the second and third innings of game two, Burdette would have matched Mathewson's record of three complete-game shutouts. As it was, he was unscored upon in the final 24 innings he pitched, a fantastic performance in its own right, if not quite a record setter.

There have been a number of other outstanding pitching performances in World Series competition, but Mathewson's great record still stands. In fact, there's never been a situation where a pitcher has thrown shutouts in his first two series games and then gone out for a third game with a chance to match Matty's record. But one pitcher who was fully capable of doing it and who turned in some incredible World Series performances was Bob Gibson of the St. Louis Cardinals.

Gibson is a Hall of Fame pitcher who won 251 games for the Cards from 1959 to 1975. No fiercer competitor ever stepped on a baseball mound than the big right-hander, who was always at his best in the biggest games. He won two games and dropped one in the 1964 World Series, but was on the mound in the decisive seventh game when the Cards won the championship. Then, in 1967, he led the Cards into another Series, this time against the Boston Red Sox.

The opener was all Gibson. Though the Red Sox managed a run in the third, the big guy shut them down on six hits and won it, 2–1. But the next day, Gibson's performance was overshadowed by that of Boston ace Jim Lonborg. Lonborg tossed a brilliant one-hit shut-out to help the Sox even the series at one game each. So it was Lonborg who had the shot at Matty's mark.

With the Cards leading two games to one, Gibson came back in game four. The Cards struck early, scor-ing four runs in the first and two in the third, and that was all Gibby needed. As was his way, he got stronger as the game wore on and shut out the Bosox, 6–0, on a five-hitter. The Cards now had a solid, 3–1 lead in games.

In the fifth game, Jim Lonborg came out and looked every bit as invincible as he had in the second contest.

Going into the ninth inning, Lonborg had a two-hit shutout. Once more, the comparisons with Matty were beginning. Then, Roger Maris broke the spell by belting a home run for the first score of the series against Lonborg. The Sox won the game, 3–1, and when they were victorious in the sixth, 8–4, it set up a seventh and deciding game.

Gibson was ready to go again, despite having just three days' rest. But the Sox were gambling. They picked Lonborg, who would be coming back with just *two* days between starts. The anticipation was great, because each pitcher had given up only one run in 18 innings of pitching. For two innings, it was scoreless, but Lonborg's fastball didn't have the same pop as it had the other two games. And in the third inning, the Cards got to him.

They scored a pair of runs, then came back with two more in the fifth and three in the sixth. Lonborg was gone, and Gibson held center stage. Though he gave up a run in the fifth and another in the eighth, he was nevertheless in command, striking out 10 and winning his third game of the series, just as Matty had done.

Gibson didn't pitch three shutouts, but he was almost as good, allowing just three runs in 27 innings while striking out 26 and walking just 5. It was an incredible performance, and, ironically, one that he came close to matching the following year.

The Cards were in the Series once again, this time facing the Detroit Tigers. In the opening game of the 1968 classic, Bob Gibson did his thing. Not only did he

A frightening sight to hitters. The Cardinals' great Bob Gibson gets set to deliver plateward with the tenacity that marked his Hall of Fame career. Gibson was always at his best in big games and was not at all reluctant to put the ball right under the batter's chin.

defeat Detroit's 31-game winner Denny McLain, but he threw a five-hit shutout in the process. And along the way he became a record breaker by striking out 17 Tigers, the most ever fanned in a World Series game.

He came back again in game four and was almost as good, throwing another five-hitter and fanning 10. But the shutout was ruined by a Jim Northrup home run in the fourth inning. So once again Christy Mathewson's record was safe. Then in the seventh game, Gibson was matched against Detroit's Mickey Lolich, who had also won a pair in the Series.

Once again Gibby looked superb, matching goose eggs with Lolich for six frames. But with two out in the seventh, a pair of singles and a fly ball (that was dropped) proved Gibson's undoing. Detroit and Lolich won the game, 4–1, and the Series. But Bob Gibson had once again pitched his heart out and emerged a record breaker. His 35 strikeouts for the series was another new mark, a mark that continues to stand.

The great performances by Lew Burdette and Bob Gibson cannot be diminished. But they point out once again what a great record Christy Mathewson set way back in 1905. For a pitcher to complete three games in a short seven-game series is an accomplishment in itself. To win those three games is an even greater feat. But to throw three shutouts in the World Series, well, that's the ultimate.

Chasing the Babe—The Home Run Story

His name was George Herman Ruth and they called him the Babe, the Bambino, the Sultan of Swat. He started out as a pitcher with the Boston Red Sox but achieved his greatest fame as an outfielder with the New York Yankees. He changed the face of baseball, almost single-handedly, by belting the ball higher and farther and more often than had ever been done before.

"Babe Ruth" means home run. That was what he did best—belt the ball out of sight. He was the cure for a game suffering the ills of the 1919 "Black Sox Scandal." Because of the attempt to fix the 1919 World Series, the game's credibility had suffered. Fans were skeptical. They needed a hero, someone to put new life into the game, someone to set some new, great records.

Ruth's timing couldn't have been better. The year was 1920, the season following the Black Sox Scandal, the year the whole story was coming out. It was also Babe Ruth's first year in New York, having come to the Yanks from the Red Sox during the offseason. All the Babe did that year was stand the baseball world on its ear by slamming 54 home runs!

To be fully understood, that achievement must be put in perspective. The year before, the Babe had set a new home-run record. He had 29. The record before that was 24, by Gavvy Cravath of the Phils in 1915. But the same year Cravath belted 24, the American League leader, Bobby Roth, had just 7. Three years later, in 1918, Cravath led the National League with just 8, while Tilly Walker of Philadelphia and a part-time outfielder for the Red Sox, George Herman Ruth, tied for the American League lead with 11 each.

It just wasn't a home-run game. Now it's referred to as the dead-ball era, because the baseball was made differently and just didn't carry as far. Then, suddenly, here comes Ruth, and out of the blue he slams 54 home runs. With the same dead ball! The National League leader that same year had just 15 round-trippers. That's how far ahead of everyone the Babe was.

When he belted 59 homers in 1921, he proved it was no fluke. And baseball knew it had a new kind of attraction. That's when they remade the baseball so it would carry further. The era of the lively ball had begun. More players began swinging from the heels and belting homers. But through it all, there was only one Babe Ruth.

The man became a legend in his own time. He was a great all-around ballplayer, as proved by his outstanding pitching mark before he became an outfielder, and his .342 lifetime batting average. But it is the home run for which he is remembered, and that was best symbolized by two great records he left behind.

There is hardly a baseball fan anywhere who doesn't

know them. The first came in 1927 when the Babe extended his own single-season mark by belting 60 home runs for the year. The second standard was the one he left behind when he retired. For the Babe slammed a total of 714 round-trippers during his long career. The two numbers became part of baseball folklore: 60 and 714. They were records many people *hoped* would never be broken.

This, then, is the story of the men who came after Babe Ruth, and what they encountered when they began chasing the records set by the greatest legend the game has ever known.

Just three years after the Babe set his record of 60, a fireplug of a player named Hack Wilson belted 56 for the Chicago Cubs, setting a National League record that still stands to this day. Wilson didn't break the Babe's mark, but he showed that it wasn't invincible. Then, two years later in 1932, a player came along who did make the first serious run at the magic mark of 60.

He was Jimmie Foxx, old "Double-X," and an outstanding slugger in his own right. Foxx finished his career with a .325 lifetime batting average and 534 home runs, so he was no slouch. He was a nineteen-year-old just beginning his career with the Philadelphia A's the year the Babe had his 60. Two years later, Foxx began to make his own presence felt in the American League as he walloped 33 home runs, drove in 117 runs, and hit .354.

Still, at the outset of the 1932 season, Jimmie Foxx had given no real indication that he was a threat to the Babe's mark. The most homers he had hit previously was 37 in 1930. But in 1932, he began belting them all over the place, and by midseason there was much speculation that he could surpass 60.

But then some strange things happened. Bad luck, and a few changes in the ballparks were part of the story. Foxx wound up with 58 home runs in 1932, but there are many baseball people who feel it very easily could have been different, that Foxx easily could have hit 63 or even 65 homers.

For one thing, he was slowed by a wrist injury in August and that led to a cool spell before he recovered to finish strongly. No injury and he might have had a couple of more right then and there. Then there was the rightfield screen in St. Louis' Sportsman's Park. They say Foxx hit it five times that year, keeping the ball in play. The screen, however, wasn't there in 1927 when the Babe hit his 60. It was put up in 1930.

There was also a screen installed in front of the leftfield bleachers in old League Park in Cleveland. This one Foxx supposedly hit at least three times. So the two screens alone might have stopped five or seven additional Foxx homers. It was almost as if the Babe's mark wasn't supposed to be beaten.

Jimmie Foxx was an outstanding slugger who again hit the 50-homer mark in 1938. Yet he played most of his career in the shadow of the Babe, and never got the full recognition he deserved. As Joe DiMaggio once said to him: "You made only one mistake, Jimmie. You were born twenty-five years too soon."

* * *

Playing for the Boston Red Sox in the twilight of his great career, Jimmie Foxx blasts his 495th home run, enabling him to pass Lou Gehrig and putting him into second place on the all-time list behind Babe Ruth. A number of modern-day players have since passed old "Double X," but he is still remembered as a great slugger and for his 58 homers in 1932.

Six years after Jimmie Foxx made his run at the Babe, another American League slugger came along to put in his bid for immortality. He was Hank Greenberg of the Detroit Tigers and his attempt to become a record breaker was also thwarted by some unusual circumstances. In fact, in some ways, Greenberg's try to top the Babe came a lot closer than Foxx's.

Hank Greenberg was a big, powerful man, standing nearly six feet, four inches tall and weighing about 215 pounds. He didn't wind up with quite the same kind of numbers as Ruth or, for that matter, Foxx. But he was still a .313 lifetime hitter, with 331 career homers to his credit. And he did this despite losing three seasons, and part of a fourth, to military service.

Greenberg had a banner year in 1937, batting .337, with 40 homers and 183 runs batted in. That was one ribby short of Lou Gehrig's American League record. So big things were still expected of him in '38. And after the season began, he started slamming home runs at a record pace.

Jimmie Foxx had come on with a brace of homers in September to close at 58, but Hank Greenberg stayed ahead of Ruth's pace. For a long time it looked as if he couldn't miss, and that baseball would have a brand new home-run king. He slammed his fifty-eighth home run with five games still remaining.

"Five games to get a pair to tie the Babe, or three to beat him. I think I can do it," Hank told friends.

The first two games were in Detroit against the old St. Louis Browns. In the first game, a wild lefthander named Howard Mills walked Hank four times. In the next game, Bobo Newsom was on the hill for the Browns. He was always tough for Hank, and this time he gave up just a single in the four times Greenberg faced him. So two of the five games had passed and the big slugger was still stalled at 58 home runs. Now it was on to Cleveland.

The first game was played at old League Park and the Tigers were facing righthander Denny Galehouse. With three games left, Greenberg might have been pressing, and Galehouse held him hitless. Then the Indians did something that probably hurt Greenberg again. They

Hank Greenberg crosses home plate after hitting still another long home run. Greenberg's 58 round-trippers in 1938 electrified the baseball world. Greeting Hank at home plate in this 1945 game is teammate Roy Cullenbine.

called off the Saturday game at League Park and decided to hold a Sunday doubleheader at the city's new stadium on Lake Erie, the huge Municipal Stadium.

It was a much larger field than League Park, with deeper dimensions in the outfield, especially in left center, Greenberg's power alley. That was one disadvantage. The second was the day itself. It was dark and dismal, with a threat of rain, not a good day for baseball. And there were no lights to turn on at the flick of a switch back then!

To pull in even more fans, the Indians started their nineteen-year-old fireballing sensation, Bob Feller, in the first game. Feller had the most fearsome fastball in the game. He had yet to get it under control, however, and that made it even more frightening to bat against him, especially on a dark day.

All Bob Feller did in the first game that day was set a new major league record with 18 strikeouts. The victims were Hank Greenberg and the Tigers, with Greenberg himself fanning twice. Still no home runs; still stalled at 58. And now there was just one game left.

In the second game the darkness continued to descend upon the stadium. Righthander Johnny Humphries was on the mound and Hank managed a pair of doubles. One of them slammed into the base of the left centerfield fence, some 420 feet away. But by the sixth inning playing conditions were worse and umpire George Moriarty finally had to call the game. Knowing what Greenberg was trying to do, the umpire sought him out.

"I'm sorry, Hank," he said. "This is as far as I can go."

A discouraged Greenberg looked up. "That's all right, George," he said. "This is as far as I can go, too."

So the man who had the best chance to top the Babe had fallen short. Hank was always proud of what he had done and said that even if he had broken the record, Ruth would always be the king of the home-run hitters. And, indeed, it was beginning to look as if the record wasn't meant to be broken.

Greenberg's try was the last real run at the Babe for a good number of years. In the 1940s, Ralph Kiner of the Pirates and Johnny Mize of the Giants both smacked 51 in 1947, and Kiner came back with 54 in 1949. But neither really made a run at 60. Then in the 1950s, a whole new group of young sluggers came into baseball.

In 1955, Willie Mays of the Giants slammed 51 homers, and a year later Mickey Mantle of the Yanks hit 52. Would either of these all-around stars challenge Ruth? Or how about Henry Aaron, Willie McCovey, Harmon Killebrew, Eddie Mathews, Orlando Cepeda, or Frank Robinson? It was a sluggers' game, and there were plenty of good ones.

The team of the 1950s and early sixties was once again the New York Yankees. As in the Babe's day, the Yanks seemed to be winning year after year, and when the 1961 season rolled around, they were heavy favorites once again. The Bombers had a power-laden lineup, featuring Mantle, Yogi Berra, Moose Skowron, Elston Howard, John Blanchard, and a strong-armed rightfielder named Roger Maris.

Maris had come to the Yanks from Kansas City in 1960, and proceeded to put together a fine season. Though missing nearly three weeks to an injury in August, he led the league with 112 RBIs and lost the home-run crown to teammate Mantle, 40–39. Yet for his all-around play, Roger Maris was the American League's Most Valuable Player for 1960.

A left-handed batter with a short, compact swing, Roger Maris wasn't considered a big slugger in the classic sense. He didn't hit the high, long, majestic homers that Mantle clouted. But his swing was perfect for the short rightfield fence at Yankee Stadium, and he hit many a line shot into the lower stands. Yet in spite of the skills of both Mantle and Maris, no one was prepared for what was about to happen in 1961.

Maris got off slowly that year, hitting around .200 during April and adding just one home run. Teammate Mantle already had seven, and all Roger Maris was thinking about was staying with the Yankees. He already expected to be traded.

"The Yankees don't keep outfielders hitting in the low .200s," he said.

Finally, in May, Maris began getting the range. At the end of the month he hit four homers in three days. As June began, Mantle had 14 and Maris 12. Yet not too many people really thought about records. But that was before they saw what happened in June.

Both outfielders began slugging the ball all over the lot. Maris really got hot. He slammed 15 that month, and when it ended he was leading Mantle, 27–25. Now, the whole baseball world was watching. Maris and Mantle, nicknamed the M-Boys, or M&M, seemed to be ready for a dual run at the longtime record held by Babe Ruth. It looked to be the most serious run since Greenberg's some twenty-three years earlier. And not one, but two players were charging after it.

That's when some of the early troubles began for

Roger Maris. Mantle was immediately the sentimental favorite. After all, the Mick was a lifetime Yankee. As the centerfielder, he was the natural successor to Ruth, Lou Gehrig, and Joe DiMaggio, the superstar who kept the line going.

Maris, on the other hand, was looked upon as an outsider, a player who was with his third team in five years. If anyone should break Ruth's record, it should be another "real" Yankee. That's the way many New York fans felt. And then halfway through the year, when both sluggers were into the mid-thirties, the baseball commissioner stepped into the fray.

Commissioner Ford Frick said that any new home-run record would have to come within the Yanks' first 154 games. That was the length of the schedule when Ruth played. In 1961, the schedule was increased to 162 games. Any record set after 154 games, would have an asterisk next to it. Many people felt this was unfair. A record should be a record, no matter what.

"I didn't even get involved in the debate," Maris said. "I still wasn't even thinking record. I just wanted to do my best and help the Yankees win another pennant."

But the M&M homer race was becoming the hottest topic of the summer, especially when neither slugger showed signs of slowing down. Mantle hit three homers at Washington, putting him ahead 36–35. The Mick held the lead into August. But four Maris homers in four games deadlocked things again at 45–45. Roger stayed hot, and within a matter of days had a 48–45 lead. Both sluggers were ahead of Ruth's pace and no one could deny the possibility of a new record.

"It became difficult for either of us to deny that the record was on our minds," Maris said. "In fact, it was on everyone's mind. We got no rest from it."

That made it more difficult for Roger Maris. An honest and straightforward man who said what he thought in no uncertain terms, Maris was never a darling of the media. And when reporters and interviewers began asking the same questions over and over, game after game, he often grew testy and uncomfortable. The daily press conference was proving a daily grind.

"I was getting embarrassed by it all," Roger admitted. "We had a lot of other guys having good years. Why not give them some attention?"

That is how Maris really felt. But he was going for a record considered almost sacred by fan and sportswriter alike. It was the sports story of the year, maybe of the decade. There was no way Roger Maris would get a rest from it. He'd have to live with it.

By mid-August there was little doubt that Mantle was the sentimental favorite. He heard the cheers, Maris the boos. The Yanks were playing to sellout crowds all around the league. Everyone wanted to see the M-Boys go for the record. And when Maris belted number 50, he became the first player ever to reach that number of home runs in August. The Babe had reached his magical 60 by slamming 17 round-trippers in September. So Maris was well ahead.

Of course, Mantle was still in it, too. When Roger

belted number 51, Mickey had 46. By the time Maris reached 53, Mantle had 48. When Roger belted number 54, he found it hard to believe it himself.

"I found myself wondering what I was doing up here with these high numbers," he said. "I never regarded myself as a home-run hitter and here I was up with the Ruths, Greenbergs, Foxxes, and Wilsons."

But he wouldn't get away from it now. Mantle belted his fifty-second on September 8, and Maris got number 56 the day after. They were already the first teammates to both hit more than 50 home runs in the same season. Now they had broken still another record, that for total homers by teammates in a season. They had 108 and counting. The old record was 107 by Ruth and Lou Gehrig in 1927.

Soon after, the team broke a record. Bill "Moose" Skowron hit one out; it was the Yanks' 222nd homer of the year, a new team mark. But nothing could divert attention from the Maris–Mantle race. Roger's fifty-seventh brought him a step closer. Then, in game 151, he whacked number 58. Mantle was stalled at 53. It was apparent now that if anyone broke the record, it would be Roger Maris. It was also apparent that Frick's asterisk would come into play.

There was so much pressure on Maris by now that his hair was falling out in chunks. It was hard to believe that he could still concentrate on baseball. But he said the only time he could relax was during the game. There was no one there to badger him or ask him the same repetitive questions about the record.

In game number 154 against Baltimore, Roger electrified the crowd by belting his fifty-ninth home run in the third inning. Could he get number 60? He struck out in the fourth, and hit a long foul in the seventh, but he couldn't get another homer. He finished the game with 59. But there were eight more games for him to break the record.

At Boston, Mantle slammed his fifty-fourth home run, but he was forced by illness to sit out the rest of the season. So Roger Maris was now on center stage. He didn't hit one in Boston, then returned to New York for the final two series against the Orioles and Red Sox. In the first game against the Orioles, Roger connected in the third inning against Jack Fisher. It was in the seats for number 60, the magic number 60. After the game, he was introduced to Mrs. Babe Ruth. Roger kissed the Babe's widow on the cheek.

"I told her that I was glad I hadn't broken the record in 154 games," he said.

Now he had four games to get his sixty-first. In the first three, he couldn't hit one out. So there was one left. Facing Boston's Tracy Stallard in the fourth inning, Roger got his pitch. One more time he used his powerful, short swing, and the ball rocketed into the lower rightfield seats. He had done it. Number 61. A new record, asterisk or not.

"As soon as I hit it I knew it was gone, number 61," he said. "It was the only time that the number of the homer ever flashed into my mind as I hit it . . . But I couldn't even think as I went around the bases. I was in

Roger Maris is about to make baseball history by cracking his 61st home run of the year against Tracy Stallard of the Boston Red Sox. The historic blast came at Yankee Stadium on October 1, 1961. The arrow shows the projected flight of the ball.

a fog. I was all fogged out from a very, very hectic season and an extremely difficult month."

That might have been an understatement. Roger Maris was a record breaker. He had broken one of baseball's more revered standards. And he paid a price few record breakers have had to pay. The media, the pressure, the people rooting against him. It's a tribute to Roger Maris that he persevered, and finally triumphed.

The same year that Roger Maris was belting his sixty-first home run, a twenty-seven-year-old outfielder with the Milwaukee Braves was completing another outstanding season in the National League. Henry Aaron, also known as Hammerin' Hank, had a .327 batting average for the year, 34 home runs and 120 RBIs. Smooth as silk at the plate, in the field, or on the basepaths, Henry Aaron could do it all and was considered one of the superstars of the game.

His 34 homers that year gave him 253 for his career, yet as a slugger, he was considered a notch below the likes of Mantle and Mays, or even Harmon Killebrew and Frank Robinson. He was thought of as a great all-around ballplayer with home-run power. Virtually no one in baseball thought of Aaron in terms of home-run records.

But as the years continued to pass, Henry Aaron kept playing his own great brand of baseball, and he continued to hit home runs with amazing consistency. In fact, he even picked up the pace. Number 300 came in April 1963. Three years later, in April 1966, he slammed number 400.

That year, the Braves franchise moved from Milwaukee to Atlanta, where the ballpark was even better suited to home runs. In July 1968, Hammerin' Hank belted number 500 off Mike McCormick of San Francisco. He was thirty-four years old then, and while he was now talked about in the same breath with Mantle and Mays, people still weren't prepared for what was to come.

Mantle had retired after the 1968 season, finishing an injury-plagued career with 536 home runs. Mays was still playing, but he was three years older than Aaron and obviously slowing down. Aaron wasn't. He belted 44 home runs in 1969 and 38 in 1970. Then, in 1971, at the age of thirty-seven, Henry Aaron had his greatest home-run year ever. He cracked 47 round-trippers to finish the year with 639 for his career.

No longer could Henry Aaron's achievements be ignored. He was not just a superb ballplayer who happened to hit a good number of home runs. He was a consistent home-run hitter who had a good chance to better the other sacred record set by Babe Ruth. That was the Babe's career record of 714 home runs.

On the night of June 10, 1972, Henry belted a grand-slam homer off Wayne Twitchell of the Phillies. It was his tenth homer of the season, but more importantly, the 649th of his career. With that round-tripper, Henry moved past the fading Mays into second place behind

A happy Henry Aaron meets the press shortly after becoming baseball's all-time home run king with 715 lifetime blasts.

the Babe. Now the chase was on. Would Hammerin' Hank be able to catch Babe Ruth?

Henry didn't have the game-to-game pressure that plagued Roger Maris in his quest for the single-season record. As long as he stayed healthy and could fight off Father Time, he had a chance. But he was also well aware of what he was trying to accomplish.

"Sure, I think about the record," Henry admitted. "I think I can do it if I stay healthy and if I have a strong man batting behind me. That way, they can't pitch around me."

Aaron finished the 1972 season with 34 home runs, giving him a career total of 673. He was now within 41 home runs of tying the Babe. And while he would be thirty-nine years old when the 1973 season began, he had taken good care of himself. He was still a fine ballplayer and a dangerous one.

Something else happened in 1972, something that would carry on as long as he chased the record. Henry began getting letters from fans. At first, they were basically polite, but had a similar theme. The writers didn't want Henry to break the record.

"They're not vicious letters," he said, "but apparently there is so much tradition and sentiment involved with Ruth's record that people don't want to see it broken.

"I guess a lot of people will be disappointed if anyone tops Ruth. But if I do it, I'll fully expect someone else to come along and top me someday."

There were other comparisons. Henry already had some 3,000 more at-bats than the Babe and his home-run-to-at-bats ratio wasn't as great. On the other hand, Ruth didn't have to play night baseball and take long, wearing plane trips. Playing conditions and the game itself change from era to era, so comparisons are merely matters for debate. A great record is a great record in any era.

Henry started the 1973 season slowly. By mid-May he had 11 homers, but his batting average was .220. Then it was learned that Henry was under pressure of another kind. The mail he was getting regarding his quest for the home-run record had turned nasty. In fact, much of it could now be classified as hate mail. And the writers had a similar theme. They didn't want a black man breaking Babe Ruth's record.

"The mail is running about 75–25 against me," Henry told the press. "Most of it is racial. They called me every bad name you can imagine. If I was white, all America would be proud of me. As far as I'm concerned, it indicates something very low in this country."

So Henry was paying an unexpected price in going after a great record. He even began to get some flak from people at the ballpark. As unfortunate as all this was, it did give Henry still more incentive to reach his goal.

"It's [the racial stuff] made me more determined than ever to break the record."

Aaron dug in. It was soon apparent that he was putting together a tremendous season for a player thirty-nine years old. And after stories of the hate mail broke, there was a ground swell of sentiment in favor of him. One poll showed that 73 percent of the people were now pulling for him to make it.

On July 21, he cracked home-run number 700 off Ken Brett of the Phillies. It was his twenty-seventh home run of the year. Then it got tougher. He hit just two home runs in the next twenty-six days. Now, to break the record in 1973, he'd need 13 homers in a little over a month. He said he didn't think he could do it.

Number 705 came on August 22, and by September

3, he had 708. On September 10, he cracked number 710, and had his batting average up to .288, the highest it had been all year. He was going to make it close, all right, and the tension continued to mount.

Number 711 came with just 10 games left. The surprising part of that was the attendance in Atlanta. Only 1,362 people watched Henry trot that one out. The Braves weren't in a pennant race, but Henry Aaron was on the brink of making history. Number 712 came five days later at the Houston Astrodome. Then Henry blasted number 713 and his fortieth of the year against lefty Jerry Reuss. But there was only one game left, and Aaron failed to hit another.

So the suspense would have to carry over to 1974. But what a year the old man had. He played in just 120 games and had just 392 at-bats. Yet 40 of his 118 hits were homers. He also drove in 96 runs and got his batting average up to .301. With all the pressure, that was amazing.

Yet Henry had always handled pressure well. He was a low-key guy, and that's one reason it took him so long to get the same recognition accorded the likes of Willie Mays and Mickey Mantle. He wasn't flashy; he was smooth. He was tense, but relaxed. In his own way, he always gave 100 percent, yet he didn't burn himself out.

So when he reported to spring training for the 1974 season, he was ready to go, in spite of his forty years and all the hoopla surrounding the impending record. The season opener was in Cincinnati, and Henry stepped in to face pitcher Jack Billingham of the Reds.

It was almost unbelievable, but Aaron jumped on Billingham's 3-1 pitch and drove it over the leftfield fence for home run number 714. It was his first swing of the season. Talk about not wasting time. Henry jogged around the bases as usual, slow and easy. But there was a slight smile on his face as his teammates greeted him at home plate.

He sat out the second game and in the third he took the collar. Then the team returned to Atlanta for its home opener against the Dodgers. In the second inning, Henry came up to face lefty Al Downing. He walked on five pitches. His second at-bat came in the fourth, and this time there was a man on base.

The first pitch was a ball. Then Downing came in with a fastball. Aaron whipped his quick wrists around and *CRACK!* The ball rocketed out to left center. The fans were on their feet, screaming. Henry watched the flight of the ball for a second, then went into his home-run trot. He had done it. Number 715. Baseball had a new home-run champion.

Henry Aaron didn't finish at 715. After completing the 1974 season with the Braves, he went over to the American League and played two seasons with the Milwaukee Brewers, serving mostly as a designated hitter. They weren't great years, but he still gave American League fans a thrill or two, and a chance to see the new home-run king.

When he retired at the end of 1976, Henry Aaron had 755 home runs, as well as a slew of other records. It was truly a Hall of Fame career.

Basking in the spotlights of Atlanta Stadium, Henry Aaron circles the bases for the 715th time. Aaron's home run off the Dodgers' Al Downing in April of 1974 enabled Bad Henry to surpass the immortal Babe Ruth's long-standing mark of 714 round-trippers.

Roger Maris and Henry Aaron. Two record breakers, two men who broke the records set by one man, George Herman Ruth. It's quite a story, and somehow, it all worked out. Roger Maris finally received the recognition and respect he deserved all along. Asterisk or no, his record is intact, without argument the most home runs hit in a season.

And Henry Aaron. He's right where he belongs; in the Hall of Fame alongside the other great players of the game. It took the easygoing Aaron awhile to get the proper recognition, but he did. He got it by being one of the most consistently outstanding ballplayers of his or any generation. And he has the records to prove it, including his 755 home runs.

As for Babe Ruth, well, he's still the Babe, the one and only. And in the minds of most baseball fans, he's still *the* home-run king, the Sultan of Swat, the man who started it all. And somehow, though they are no longer the all-time records, his numbers still have a magic ring: 60 home runs in a season, 714 for a career. They mean as much as they ever did.

A happy ending all around.

A Few More One-Shots

Not all records are long, drawn-out affairs. Some come quickly and without warning, and you can even chuckle at them a bit. They're more or less offbeat records, not as important as, say, the home-run record, or a strikeout mark, or a hitting streak. But they're records nevertheless.

Phil Niekro and Steve Carlton are no strangers to records. The two veteran hurlers are both ticketed for the Hall of Fame after they retire. But at the beginning of 1987, they were both continuing their great careers.

Niekro began his career with the Milwaukee Braves back in 1964. A master of the knuckleball, he has aged gracefully and continued as an effective pitcher. Because the flutterball doesn't put a great deal of strain on the arm, Niekro entered his twenty-fourth big-league season in 1987 . . . at the age of forty-eight! He began the season with the Cleveland Indians.

As for Steve Carlton, he began with St. Louis back in 1965, so he's in his twenty-third season. Unlike Niekro,

Carlton has always been a power pitcher, relying on a fastball and wicked slider for his success, most of which came with his tenure at Philadelphia. He was a great pitcher and a record breaker in Philly, winning four Cy Young Awards, the most of anyone, among many other things.

But as of opening day 1987, Steve Carlton was also in Cleveland, a teammate of Phil Niekro's. Despite his forty-two years, Carlton wanted to continue pitching and the Indians gave him the chance. But what about the record he shares with Niekro?

It happened on April 9, 1987, in a game at Toronto. Niekro started it and went five innings, eventually getting the victory. The man who relieved and went the final four? None other than Steve Carlton. And the record? Well, the occasion marked the first time two 300-game winners had ever appeared together on the same team in the same game.

The victory went to Niekro, the 312th of his great career. And the save went to Carlton. But before he started saving games, he had won 323 of them on his own. So together, these two great veterans were responsible for 635 wins. And they were still counting.

Frank Robinson was a great player and a record breaker. As a rookie with the Cincinnati Reds in 1956, he tied a record for a first-year player by slamming 38 home runs. When he retired after the 1976 season, he had 586 round-trippers, which made him the fourth-best home-run hitter in baseball history.

So Frank Robinson was a star for his entire career. In 1961, he led the Reds to the National League pennant and for his efforts was named the National League's Most Valuable Player. But four years later he was involved in a very controversial trade. The Reds shipped him to the Baltimore Orioles of the American League, claiming he was "an old thirty."

Oh, did he ever prove them wrong. In his first year with the Orioles, all Frank Robinson did was win the American League Triple Crown, lead the Birds to a pennant and World Series victory, and find himself named the A. L.'s Most Valuable Player. That gave him still another record as the only man ever to win the MVP prize in both leagues.

Of course, no matter where Frank Robinson played, he hit home runs. Not enough to top Henry Aaron, Babe Ruth, and Willie Mays, the three players ahead of him on the all-time list, but enough to make him a record-breaking slugger.

For starters, Frank Robinson is the only player in big-league history to hit more than 200 homers in each league. He belted 343 in the National League, and another 243 in the American. That's not all. Robby is also the only player to hit home runs for both the National and American leagues in All-Star Games. He did it for the N.L. in 1959, and for the A.L. in 1971.

Robinson also shares a unique home-run record with Rusty Staub. Each homered in 32 different major league ballparks during their careers. So it didn't much matter to Frank Robinson where he played. As long as

Baltimore's great slugger Frank Robinson setting a new record as he belts his 10th home run during the month of April in 1969. Robby was a record breaker in other ways as well. He is the only player to win the MVP Award in both leagues and the only player to hit more than 200 home runs in both the National and American Leagues.

the ballpark had a fence, Robby would hit the baseball over it.

What is the safest way for a pitcher to assure himself a victory? Easy. Pitch a shutout. But it's easier said than done. A pitcher must have his best stuff and get the breaks to boot. There once was a pitcher, however, who made a career of pitching shutouts. He was Walter Johnson, the Big Train, and one of the greatest hurlers who ever lived.

Johnson pitched for the old Washington Senators from 1907 to 1927, winning 416 games during his career. In all of baseball history, only Cy Young won more. But playing for the Senators, Johnson often didn't have much support. There was an old joke about the Washington franchise that held a real ring of truth during much of Johnson's career. It went like this:

Washington—first in war, first in peace, and *last* in the American League!

Because of a lack of support, Walter Johnson lost a lot of close games. The safest route for him to go was to pitch a shutout, a lesson he learned early and took to heart. For in his career, Walter Johnson set a major league record by throwing 113 shutouts. That's amazing. He blanked the opposition in more than one-fourth of his victories.

Just to prove how badly the Big Train sometimes needed a shutout, one need only look at the following statistic. On 64 different occasions, Walter Johnson was involved in 1–0 ballgames. He won 38 of them. The other 26 were heartbreaking defeats. No wonder he was a record-breaking shutout pitcher. He had to be.

Another Hall of Fame hurler also made his mark via the whitewash. He was Grover Cleveland Alexander, winner of 373 games from 1911 to 1930. Alex, as he was called, threw 90 shutouts in his lifetime, a National League standard and second only to Walter Johnson on the all-time list.

But Alexander holds one shutout mark all by himself. During the 1916 season, while en route to a brilliant, 33–12 record, Alex was a threat every time he

107

went to the mound. He took every run he yielded as a personal affront. But he didn't yield many. On 16 different occasions, Grover Cleveland Alexander went to the mound and came off a shutout winner. That's a record that has stood the test of time right to this day.

There was another shutout record held by Walter Johnson that also looked rather invincible when he set it. From April 10 to May 14, 1913, the Big Train racked up 55⅔ straight scoreless innings. It was a standard that also stood the proverbial test of time, that is, until 1968, when a tall righthander for the L.A. Dodgers wiped it out.

His name was Don Drysdale, a six-six fireballer who won over 200 games during his career. By 1968, however, the Big D was struggling. He had losing seasons in both 1966 and '67, and it was obvious that his best days were behind him. But suddenly, for a three-week period in May and early June of 1968, Don Drysdale was as good as any pitcher who ever lived.

On May 14, Drysdale cranked it up and threw a shutout, a tight, 1–0 victory over the Chicago Cubs. On May 18, he did it again, whitewashing the Astros by that same, tight, 1–0 score. There was life in his aging arm yet. Then on May 22, Drysdale went up against the St. Louis Cardinals. This time his Dodger teammates got him two runs. But he only needed one. That's right, he pitched another shutout, winning it by a 2–0 score.

Three straight shutouts, a worthy achievement. But it couldn't last forever. The next time out it was the Astros again on May 26. They should have learned something last time, but apparently they didn't. Drysdale shut them out for a second time, 5–0, for his fourth consecutive blanking.

Now it was the Giants' turn to try to solve Drysdale. Their turn came on May 31, but they had no better luck than the four previous opponents. You guessed it, still another shutout, this one by a 3–0 count. That was five straight, tying a major league record and giving the Big D 45 straight scoreless innings. By now, the whole baseball world was watching.

Even the usually cool Drysdale must have felt the butterflies when he went up against the Pittsburgh Pirates on June 4. But once he started throwing, everything was just fine. He had the good stuff again, the super stuff, and he set the Bucs down inning after inning. When it ended, Drysdale and the Dodgers had still another shutout, winning by a 5–0 count.

So Drysdale was now a record breaker, his six straight shutouts giving him a new mark. It also gave him 54 straight scoreless innings, and Walter Johnson's long-standing record was within reach. Could Drysdale do it one more time?

His next start was on June 8, against the Phillies. When Drysdale pitched through the first two innings without allowing a run, he had tied the record. Then he went out for the third frame, and retired the Phillies once again. He had done it, cracked the Johnson record by pitching his fifty-seventh straight scoreless inning. The next inning he extended it to 58. Then it ended.

In the fifth, with two on and one out, pinch hitter Howie Bedell hit a sacrifice fly to score Tony Taylor with a run. Drysdale and the Dodgers went on to win the game, 5–3, but one of the hottest pitching streaks in baseball history had come to an end. The 58⅔ scoreless innings thrown by Drysdale remains a record to this day.

Don Drysdale finished the 1968 season with a very mediocre 14–12 mark. He would pitch just part of one more season before arm problems would force him to call it quits. Yet in the twilight of his career, Don Drysdale turned back the clock and set an amazing record. The great ones often find a way to do that.

Strikeouts. They can be dramatic. The big, power pitcher standing tall on the mound, ready to challenge the hitter with his best stuff. Some fans may prefer to see home runs sailing high and long out of the park. But a power pitcher blowing away hitter after hitter, especially in the late innings, is quite an imposing sight as well.

The interesting thing is that most of the great strikeout records are held by great pitchers, whether they be game, season, or career marks. Those who set the records as well as those who broke them all have their own special niche in baseball history.

On July 30, 1933, a big righthander for the St. Louis Cardinals took the mound against the Chicago Cubs in the first game of a doubleheader. The big guy enjoyed pitching and winning, and when he had his strikeout pitch going, he like to say he "fogged" one right past the batter.

His name was Jay Hanna Dean, but everyone called him Dizzy. And ol' Diz was one of the great pitchers of his time. Though his career was shortened by injury, he nevertheless won 150 games, most of them coming during a six-year stretch, and is a member of baseball's Hall of Fame.

Diz is often remembered for his zany antics as well as his pitching, but in the first game of the doubleheader with the Cubs he was all pitcher. When the smoke had cleared, ol' Diz had fogged enough fastballs through there to strike out 17 Cubs. It was a major league record, but even Dizzy Dean probably knew it wouldn't last forever.

It lasted five years, until late in the 1938 season. Then it was broken by a strong-armed, nineteen-year-old kid named Bob Feller. Feller was to acquire the nickname, "Rapid Robert," because he was the hardest thrower of his day, a strikeout pitcher who was just wild enough to strike the right amount of fear in the hearts of opposing batters. Feller wound up his career as a record breaker and the winner of some 266 ballgames. He also left behind a big *what if?*

You see, Bob Feller lost almost four full seasons to the military during World War II—seasons during which he undoubtedly would have averaged 25 or more victories. He could have easily had another hundred wins and maybe 1,000 more strikeouts to add to his total of 2,581.

As it was, Bob Feller didn't waste much time making his presence felt in the American League. He was just nineteen years old in 1938 and already making a reputation. And he solidified it on the final day of the season, pitching the first game of a doubleheader at huge Municipal Stadium in Cleveland.

That was the day Hank Greenberg of the Tigers still had an outside shot at Babe Ruth's record of 60 homers. Greenberg came in with 58, but it was a dark, dismal day in Cleveland, and the weather favored the flame-throwing Feller. All he did that afternoon was break Dizzy Dean's single-game strikeout mark. Feller fanned 18 Tigers, including Greenberg twice, to become a record breaker for the first time in his career. It wouldn't be the last. We'll hear from him again.

As for his 18-strikeout record, it endured. It wasn't until twenty-one years later that a pitcher came along to tie it. And it was another great one, Sandy Koufax of the Dodgers, a classy lefthander who averaged more than a strikeout an inning during his entire career.

By now the Koufax story is well known. As a hard-throwing young lefthander who couldn't get his game under control, Koufax struggled for six years before he found the secret. On the advice of catcher Norm Sherry, Koufax began to relax on the mound, throwing easier and with a more fluid motion instead of trying to overpower every pitch. And he blossomed.

In the final six years of his career, Koufax was as overpowering and dominant as any pitcher ever. Like

Dizzy Dean before him, he was forced to retire prematurely due to an injury. In fact, his final season, 1966, might have been his best. He was 27–9 with a 1.73 earned run average and 317 strikeouts.

Like most great power pitchers, Sandy Koufax seemed to get stronger as the game wore on, and he often stood tall on the mound in the final innings, blowing away one hitter after another. And on two separate occasions, he tied Bob Feller's mark by striking out 18 batters in the game.

The first time was on August 31, 1959, against the San Francisco Giants. As usual, he came on late, getting two in the seventh, two in the eighth, and all three Giants in the ninth to reach 18. He duplicated the feat on April 24, 1962, against the Chicago Cubs. But for a man who threw four no-hitters, including a perfect game, won three Cy Young Awards, and set several other strikeout marks, it wasn't surprising. What was surprising was that he didn't do it more often.

So the record stood at 18 until 1969. Then it was broken, and the new record breaker was another great pitcher, Steve Carlton. Lefty, as he is called, would go on to win more than 300 games and a record four Cy Young Awards. He spent the most productive years of his career with the Philadelphia Phillies, but when he first made history in 1969, he was with the St. Louis Cardinals.

It was his fifth year in the league and on the night of September 15, he got the call against the New York Mets, who were on the way to their first National

League title ever. But that night, Carlton had his good fastball and outstanding slider, and he began fanning Mets. However, in the fourth inning Mets' rightfielder Ron Swoboda got his pitch and belted a two-run homer.

Carlton shook it off and continued to strike out Mets at a clip that would give him a shot at the record. Then in the eighth, with the Cards leading 3–2, Swoboda came up again with a man on base. As unbelievable as it seems, the rightfielder connected for a second, two-run homer, giving the Mets the lead at 4–3.

That didn't deter Carlton. With two out in the ninth, he had tied the Feller–Koufax record at 18. Mets' outfielder Amos Otis was up. Sure enough, Carlton bore down and fanned Otis. He had set a new single-game strikeout record with 19! But when the Cards couldn't score in the bottom of the ninth, Steve Carlton suffered the final irony of a record-breaking performance. He lost the game!

On April 22, 1970, Tom Seaver of the New York Mets received an award. He was presented with the Cy Young Award as the best pitcher of 1969. That year, Seaver had a 25–7 record and had pitched the amazing Mets to a pennant and World Series triumph. And it was no fluke. Seaver would go on to win another pair of Cy Youngs as well as more than 300 games in his illustrious career. He would also set a major league record by striking out 200 or more batters for 9 consecutive seasons.

After receiving his prize on that April afternoon,

Seaver took to the Shea Stadium mound in New York to face the San Diego Padres. The strong righthander had his good stuff and was setting down the Padres with little trouble. With two out in the sixth inning, Seaver already had nine strikeouts. Then he fanned the final hitter for number ten.

In the seventh, Seaver really began firing his fastball. He struck out all three men to face him. Then, he did it again in the eighth. Suddenly, the crowd at Shea Stadium was roaring, and word went on the teletype all over the league. Tom Seaver was within one strikeout of tying the record of eight consecutive strikeouts, a mark held by four different pitchers. And he was within three strikeouts of Carlton's record 19, set just seven months earlier.

Seaver took the mound in the ninth and went to work. The first Padre hitter was third baseman Van Kelly. Still firing as hard as he had in the first, maybe even harder, Seaver fanned Kelly to tie the record. He then faced the dangerous Clarence Gaston. The result was the same and the crowd roared. The Mets' righty had struck out his ninth in a row, a new record. And he now had 18 for the game.

With Al Ferrara coming up, Seaver took a deep breath. Ferrara had homered earlier in the game for the Padres only run, and with a 2–1 lead, Seaver didn't want to give up another gopher. He bore down. This time Ferrara couldn't touch him. He went down swinging and Seaver had done it. He was a record breaker on his own with 10 straight strikeouts, and he joined Steve

Carlton with his total of 19 whiffs for the game. Who would be next?

While Carlton and Seaver were setting their records, there was another strikeout pitcher on the horizon, if only he'd be given a chance. His name was Nolan Ryan, and he joined the New York Mets for the first time in 1966 as a nineteen-year-old. Ryan had a blazing fastball, but he couldn't control it, and with the Mets he never got the chance to put it together. For five years the New Yorkers shifted Ryan from the bullpen and back to starting, or to the bench for a while.

One of the most amazing pitchers of all time is Nolan Ryan of the Houston Astros. Ryan holds a brace of strikeout records, including 383 for a season and more than 4,500 for his career. But perhaps the most amazing thing of all is that past the age of 40, Ryan continues to throw a fastball clocked in the mid-90s. In 1987, he once again led the majors with 270 K's.

Finally, they shipped him to the California Angels in 1972, and once there, Ryan got the ball and pitched. And along the way he became the greatest strikeout pitcher who ever lived. His blazing fastball has never left him, even as he pitched into his fortieth year in 1987. Add to that a sharp breaking curve and occasional changeup, and Ryan can be unhittable, as his major-league-record five no-hitters will attest.

Already a record breaker by 1974, Ryan joined the select company of Steve Carlton and Tom Seaver. He struck out 19 batters in a single game, the first American Leaguer to do so. Now, the question was, would anybody reach 20?

It took another twelve years after 1974, but it happened. On April 29, 1986, a young righthander for the Boston Red Sox named Roger Clemens took to the mound to face the Seattle Mariners at Fenway Park in Boston. Clemens had already won his first three starts, and the usually skeptical Boston fans began to think the team might have a new ace.

Clemens wasn't a rookie, but he had limited major league experience, and had undergone arm surgery the season before. But he was a big, strong pitcher with a blazing fastball. In other words, he could bring it. And bring it he did against the Mariners. He started by striking out five of the first six Mariners he retired and took it from there. When the smoke cleared in the ninth inning, Roger Clemens had set a brand-new record, 20 strikeouts in a single game!

So the line continues. Dean to Feller to Koufax to

Boston's Roger Clemens raises his arms in triumph after striking out a record 20 Seattle Mariners on April 29, 1986.

Carlton to Seaver to Ryan to Clemens. Will Roger Clemens justify his place with these other strikeout kings? He's off to a great start. His 20K game made him 4–0 on the season, and he ran it to 14–0 before suffering his first loss.

When the season ended, Roger Clemens had a 24–4 record, had pitched the Red Sox to a divisional title and into the playoffs, and eventually walked off with both the Cy Young Award and Most Valuable Player prize. Now he must do something even more difficult. That is, keep his quality pitching up over a long period of time. The others sure did. Listen to how the same names keep cropping up in relation to the other big strikeout records.

In 1904, a pitcher named Rube Waddell set a record by fanning 343 batters. That record stood until 1946 when Bob Feller fanned 348. It was thought then that Feller's achievement would be untouchable.

Not with the great modern-day strikeout pitchers. In 1965, a year before an elbow injury forced his retirement, Sandy Koufax blew away the record. He fanned 382 batters in 335⅔ innings for a brand-new mark. How long would this one last?

The answer is eight years. Then there was still another record-breaking performance. This one was by that man again, Nolan Ryan. In 1973, Ryan upped the record to 383, topping Koufax by one strikeout. And he did it in the final game of the year, a game which fortunately for Ryan, went 11 innings. And even with the extra frames, Ryan had to fan 16 Minnesota hitters to break the record. Well, he did it.

Ryan also shattered another Koufax mark. Sandy had reached the 300-strikeout plateau on three different occasions. Ryan has done it five times! An amazing achievement. Of course, had Koufax not been injured and retired at thirty-one, well . . .

As for career whiffs, for years and years the standard was 3,508 strikeouts, set by the great Walter Johnson. In fact, no other pitcher had ever surpassed 3,000 strikeouts besides Johnson. That didn't stand up to the modern-day fireballers.

At the end of the 1987 season, Nolan Ryan had the incredible total of 4,547 strikeouts! He just walked away from Johnson. He also has the record for games in which he struck out 10 or more batters. And he's still throwing fastballs for the Houston Astros. So his record will go even higher.

But he's not the only one. Steve Carlton has also topped the 4,000 strikeout barrier. Tom Seaver surpassed 3,500. The same names. So have a number of other modern pitchers topped 3,000, veteran hurlers such as Don Sutton, Gaylord Perry, and Bob Gibson. Koufax and Bob Feller would have done it if their careers hadn't been interrupted by injury and the military.

But that's all part of the game. The various strikeout records have certainly been the private domain of some very great pitchers. No one-shot heroes here. Only Hall of Famers and future Hall of Famers. So a pitcher like Roger Clemens has something to shoot for. He's already set a record that puts him in some very select company. But he's got to keep doing it if he wants to be mentioned in the same breath with the others. The strikeout artists. They're special, all right, as well as being part of baseball's record breakers.

About the Author

BILL GUTMAN has been an avid sports fan ever since he can remember. A free-lance writer for fourteen years, he has done profiles and bios of many of today's sports heroes. Although Mr. Gutman likes all sports, he has written mostly about baseball and football. Currently, he lives in Poughquag, New York, with his wife and two step-children.